THE LOST NAZI GOLD TRAIN

ARMAND ROSAMILIA

SEVEREDPRESS

THE LOST NAZI GOLD TRAIN

WWW.SEVEREDPRESS.COM

ISBN: 978-1-923165-68-7

CHAPTER ONE

1945. Owl Mountains, Poland.

Oberst Adler Koch was growing impatient. *This should have been done already, the tracks torn up, the tunnels sealed*, he thought.

They were running out of time and this was the one task he'd been assigned in the past month. If he failed…

Koch shook his head. He would not fail. That was unthinkable. He'd do what needed to be done for Germany, for his homeland. He'd make this work.

Another plane flew overhead but it was too high in the sky to make out if it was one of theirs or the damn Russians again, on another bombing raid.

"Hurry, hurry. We're running out of daylight," the Oberst yelled from where he sat on the top of his vehicle, an umbrella blocking the sun's rays. He had bad skin and burned easily.

The prisoners were ripping up the train tracks, piling the rail ties onto the trucks. Clearing all traces of the way the armored train had gone within the last hour.

Koch radioed his second in command and asked for an update.

"The train is secured. We've made sure there is no exit except the one we came in on, and we've wired it.

As soon as we clear out the workers and our men we'll blast it and hide the train," the man said.

"Do nothing until I arrive." Koch waved for his driver. "We will go down the track now. Hurry."

As they drove, Koch admired the dozens of men who were busy tearing up the tracks and clearing away the debris. Not all of them were prisoners of war. He had a loyal group of men with him. They might not have strength in numbers but they were all good men.

Koch almost felt bad for what he had to do, but such was life and war.

His second was standing in the mouth of the tunnel when Koch arrived.

"We're set to go. We just need to radio down and let them know to exit quickly."

Koch nodded. "I need you to go down there personally and make sure every last one of them gets out. I also want to make sure no one has taken anything with them. Do you understand?"

His second looked worried but nodded. "As you command."

Koch watched as the man began to jog into the tunnel. He noted where the wires were running to and saw the man at the controls, smoking a cigarette and waiting for his orders.

If this goes right, we will have secured over three hundred tons of gold, jewelry and artwork for our Fuhrer. Enough to rebuild if we actually lose the war, Koch thought.

"Commander, can you hear me? We have a problem. The men are dead. All of them. I don't understand what is happening. Dear Lord, is that…" The radio squawked a couple of times before Koch, frustrated, turned it off. He didn't have time for this nonsense.

Koch walked over to the man and told him to put out his cigarette and blow the tunnel. Now.

"But, Commander, there are men inside–"

Koch frowned. He pulled his Luger P08 and put it to the man's temple. "I am giving you a direct order."

The man nodded, stamped his cigarette into the dirt, and stomped on the controller. There was a two-second pause before the dull sound of explosions could be heard and the ground shook underfoot. A series of blasts began getting closer to where Koch stood and he feared he'd be killed, but the tunnel mouth collapsed and the explosions stopped.

"All those men," the man said, taking his cigarettes out again and looking like he was going to cry.

Koch shot the man in the head before he could light his cigarette.

He turned and walked back to his car. "Drive me back and have your weapon ready. As soon as the last of the tracks are removed we will need to kill all of the prisoners and bury their bodies."

Koch wished they'd been quicker because he could've marched them into the tunnel and let them die, buried inside.

He sat under his umbrella and waited for the railroad ties to be put onto the truck before he gave the order to kill everyone not in a Nazi uniform.

CHAPTER TWO

Present Day. London, England.

"This can't be real. They've dug up half of Poland looking for the Wałbrzych Gold Train. It is a myth, a rumor that has no merit. You're wasting your time." Dieter Stanek wanted nothing more than to get drunk on the fine bottle of gin his friend had brought him.

Emilia Wagner shook her head. "I brought you the gin so you'd get drunk and at least amuse me, acting like you thought it was worthwhile."

"But it is not. Surely you see this." Dieter filled his glass again. "This is a fine spirit, which I thank you for."

"I picked up a couple of bottles when I was in Poland last week," Emilia said with a smile. "Scouting for where we'll be digging in a couple of weeks. I'd like you to join the expedition."

"Expedition? Bah. This is a fool's errand." Dieter took a sip of gin and smacked his lips. "I'm enjoying my retirement, anyway. Nothing better than having nothing better to do than have a mid afternoon drink followed by a long nap."

"Old man, I need you on this. Like old times," Emilia said. She knew that might stir Dieter up, since he was only a year older than her. He acted much older, more like their parents, but she was always positive.

At thirty-five, she felt she had most of her life ahead of her. A life she wanted to fill with adventures. Dieter, on the other hand, acted like he had one foot in the grave.

She supposed their different upbringings had done that, too.

They'd met at Harvard University when both were enrolled in their archeology program. Emilia wanted to be the seeker of truth and history, while Dieter wanted to be the real-life Indiana Jones.

"I am an old man," Dieter said, putting down his gin. "I no longer seek exciting times. I'm not interested in getting covered in dust and touching mummified remains. The thought of gold and silver no longer concerns me." He smiled. "I have everything I need right here. A full library and a full bar. A maid and a butler. Thousands of hours of television shows and movies to watch. All the classical music that has ever been recorded at my fingertips."

Emilia chuckled. "Please tell me you're listening to classical music because you're trying to get with some woman."

Dieter winked. "Obviously. Why else would I listen to that boring stuff? Her name is Maria. From Spain, teaching here in London. We met through a mutual friend. She also has money, more than she could ever spend."

So did Dieter. His parents had come from money. Generational money, too. His parents had never given him anything he hadn't earned, which always impressed

Emilia. He had to pay his own way through Harvard, even though his family were multimillionaires.

"I need you," Emilia said in her whining, pleading voice she knew her friend could never resist. "One last adventure and then I will never bother you again."

Dieter frowned. "You are such a bad liar. No."

Emilia pouted another few seconds before throwing up her hands. "Fine. I'll let her know you're not interested. I'm sure I can find someone else from my past."

Dieter sat up and frowned. "Don't you dare–"

"Rolf would help. He's liked me since freshman orientation." Emilia didn't even know how to contact Rolf and had no desire to see the man ever again, but Dieter didn't know that.

"I'm calling your bluff on Rolf," Dieter said. "Now… who's the woman?"

Emilia smiled. She had him. "Greta Hagar. Remember her?"

Now Dieter was grinning. "How could I forget the lovely Greta? Next time lead with that. Fine, I'm in. When do we leave?"

"In three days," Emilia said. "Do you need me to send a car for you?"

Dieter snorted. "At this point I own all of the car services in London. Sending me one of my own cars seems strange. Text me the details and I'll see you and Greta soon."

Emilia left, happy Dieter was going to help her on this adventure.

Now all she needed to do was talk to Greta Hagar and convince her to join them, even though Emilia knew the woman despised Dieter.

CHAPTER THREE

Hans Koch had been up all night, unable to sleep. He'd heard through the grapevine about an expedition to find the hidden treasure, and he knew that could never happen.

His grandfather had helped to hide the loot over seventy-five years ago. He'd only spoken about it when he was much older. In the year before he died he'd told Hans it was his one regret in life.

"I let those men die in the tunnel. I had a man set off the charges and kill all of them," Grandfather Adler had told him one night when they were alone. "And… I'll never forget what my second-in-command said before the tunnel was blown."

Commander, can you hear me? We have a problem. The men are dead. All of them. I don't understand what is happening. Dear Lord, is that…

Adler Koch had been an imposing figure, even to his last breath. He never smiled, never talked about the war. Never told anyone he loved them or hugged a family member.

He was the pillar, the rock in the center of the family, the one who ruled with an iron fist, even into his later years.

Everyone knew he was a Nazi. There'd been rumors about what he'd done during the war. What atrocities he'd witnessed and/or committed.

No one asked him about it. No one ever wanted to know about his life in South America after the war, either. He returned to Germany and settled in Austria in 1949. Met a local woman and got married. Began having children. Owned a farm, a sizable one.

No one asked him where the money came from to purchase such a large farm, one of the biggest dairies in the country.

In those days you didn't ask about the war, and as time passed you tried to forget about your relative's part in all of it. You went on with your day and acted like the Holocaust had never occurred, and certainly not by the hands of a blood relative.

Hans had never looked into it, not too much. As he got older he began to wonder what his grandfather meant about burying men in a tunnel.

The Gold Train was a myth. Nothing more. A story told about the might of the Third Reich, hiding treasure to rebuild and form the Fourth Reich in the future.

Hans followed the news as he grew about a handful of Nazi leaders spotted in South America, about sporadic arrests and trials.

His own grandfather had simply come back to Europe and started a new life as a farmer. He hadn't even tried to change his name.

No one ever questioned Hans about his family. No one in Austria wanted to talk about it, to rehash what had happened two generations ago.

His parents had been racist, that much was certain. They'd never instilled in their son their hate of non-Aryan people, but they never hid it too well, either.

Hans had studied abroad, first in Japan and then in the United States. His ancient history and German language degrees didn't amount to much actual work, but the family money would carry him through as well as several more generations.

Because of Adler Koch, the Koch family would never be poor.

The fact the money had likely been procured because it was stolen from Polish families as well as the Jews and the Gypsies didn't sit well with Hans, but there was no paper trail to figure out where it had come from.

His goal was to give back in any way possible. He anonymously donated to many charities for restitution. He spent his free time searching for treasures that could be given back to their rightful owner.

Now, with the rumor of the Nazi Gold Train and a team trying to locate it yet again… Hans had a pit in his stomach.

What if it was actually found, and the bodies of those poor workers along with it? Could it be traced back to Adler Koch?

CHAPTER FOUR

Greta Hagar nearly laughed Emilia Wagner out of her posh apartment, before shrugging her shoulders and asking if Emilia wanted tea.

"Tea would be lovely."

Greta waved at the couches. "Then sit and I'll have someone fetch it for us. Then we can gossip for a bit before I show you to the door, never to darken my doorstep with the name Dieter Stanek again."

Emilia knew this was a crapshoot, and a longshot for Greta to want anything to do with this adventure, especially if Dieter was a part of it.

After they'd sat in silence for a few minutes and received their tea, Emilia put on her best smile. "Look, Greta, I know you and Dieter don't exactly get along, but–"

Greta laughed. "Is that what you think this is about? Dieter and I had a spat, or I have no real reason to like the man? Hardly, I assure you. There is a history there that would take hours to explain, and even then I don't believe anyone would understand or believe it."

"I'd like to hear it," Emilia said. If there was any hope of Greta joining them, everything needed to be on the table. All issues put behind them.

Greta shook her head. "I'm not interested in anything that man touches. Especially if he thinks he can touch me."

Emilia frowned. Had there been sexual harassment? Had her good friend Dieter made an unwanted advance on Greta… or something even worse?

Greta chuckled. "I see by the look on your face you think the worst. No, no, nothing like that. If Dieter was ever foolish enough to do or say anything untoward, I would simply punch his lights out. He doesn't scare me physically, and mentally I run rings around the man."

"Tell me. Please," Emilia said. She desperately wanted to know.

At first, Emilia didn't think Greta was going to say another word about it. She'd taken a sip of tea.

"Fine. He stole from me." Greta looked pained.

Emilia gasped. "What did he take?"

"I wrote a paper on the historical account of the beginnings, the true beginnings, of World War I and World War II," Greta said. "It took me months. A lot of research. I made the mistake of getting drunk one night and telling Dieter all about it."

Emilia put up her hand. "Wait… didn't Dieter write a similar paper, getting his first grant to study in Poland?"

Greta was staring at Emilia. "He stole my notes when I passed out. Copied them, if nothing else. Swore he had a similar idea he'd been working on at the time."

"You thought he was lying," Emilia said.

"I don't think, I know. He had some very similar ideas. The same theories I went through, so did he. In fact, we came to the same conclusions," Greta said. She took another sip of tea. "By the time I finished my paper and submitted it, it was too late. Dieter became the talk of the historical community with his work. I was looked down upon, as if I stole *his* idea."

Emilia didn't know any of this. She'd heard Dieter talking about his paper and how excited he was, but had never heard Greta was doing something similar. The women weren't good friends and had never been, only knowing one another because of their mutual friend, Dieter.

The women finished their teas and Emilia stood, extending her hand. "I thank you for your time, Greta. I hope we can see one another again once I return from Poland."

"Poland, eh? You never did tell me what you were searching for." Greta smiled. "Once you brought up Dieter, knowing my feelings, I shut you down. I'm sorry for that. Might as well tell me what you're going to be looking for, and then I'll see you to the door."

"Wałbrzych Gold Train," Emilia said.

Greta slowly smiled. "Do you believe it is more than a myth, a rumor circulated to keep the Polish government searching fruitlessly through the mountains?"

"I do."

Greta chuckled. "And Dieter thinks so, too?"

"Yes, he does." Emilia didn't tell Greta she was more sure about it being real than Dieter, but didn't want to let Greta know this.

"Then I'm in. You will run interference between me and Dieter. How many workers will you need from me, as well as supplies? I've always been interested in the search for treasures stolen by the Nazi scum," Greta said and shook Emilia's hand.

CHAPTER FIVE

Dieter Stanek needed to get a couple of people off of his back before he could, in all good conscience, enjoy this new and exciting expedition.

He was also troubled his past would not only catch up with him, but interfere with Emilia and the search for Nazi treasure.

If I can just clear half a million dollars worth of treasure, I'll be set, Dieter thought.

Luckily, he only owed about half that much to his debtors, but he knew he'd eventually gamble more and lose more.

Dieter knew what he was doing was wrong, but so far he'd been ahead of it. So he'd thought, anyway. While the debt had continued to creep up to monumental heights, the man he was into for a lot of money had never pushed too hard to collect.

Until it had reached five hundred thousand dollars. Money Dieter didn't have easy access to. He'd occasionally paid a few thousand here and there whenever Mister Moody had messaged or called. The man would send a couple of his London-based men to collect. While they usually frowned and didn't string more than three words together, they were at least respectful and took the payment from Dieter without threats of broken legs.

Mister Moody's demeanor had changed in the last couple of weeks. Now he wanted a bigger chunk of the money, and he said the vig was continuing to grow.

Dieter had to Google what the word vig meant, and it was as he suspected: interest on the money. At an exorbitant amount, too.

He'd just gotten off of the phone with Mister Moody and the man was not happy. Even though he was in Boston in the United States, his reach extended across the ocean.

"I want my money," Mister Moody had said. "When will you pay me back?"

"Very soon. I promise." Dieter thought it was enough, since in the past it had always been good enough to keep Mister Moody at bay. Not this time.

"I need a date. The vig is growing with each day, and I've extended you too far. I want U.S. dollars as always. You need to figure this out." Mister Moody had sighed. "I don't want to threaten you, Stanek. I don't run my business that way. So be it… I will if I don't have money in hand and soon."

"I understand," Dieter had said. "I'm going to get it to you in full very soon."

"Full, huh? Are you going to rob a bank? I hear the cops don't carry guns over there," Mister Moody said.

"I have a thing I'll be working on in Poland."

"Robbing a bank in Poland? Sounds sketchy." Mister Moody laughed at his joke.

Dieter laughed. "No, no. Ever hear of the legend of the Nazi treasure train? We're looking for that."

"Ooh, that sounds interesting. That would definitely clear your debt with me and then some. I'll have to Google that," Mister Moody said.

Dieter knew he'd said too much. If Mister Moody thought there was even more to collect than his half a million, he might send some goons around to make sure he got more than was owed.

I am an idiot, Dieter thought.

He rushed to get off the phone and worried for the rest of the day. When he'd gone out to get dinner, he was sure he was being followed. Dieter made sure to lock his door and windows.

When Emilia called it was a nice distraction before bed.

"Are you ready to go? I fly out in the morning and you'll meet me in two days," she said. "And… Greta will be there, too."

Dieter groaned. "Why?"

"I thought you wanted her there. She will be invaluable."

"I know, but… I didn't think she'd want to come. I thought… forget it. I guess we'll deal with it when it happens, right?" Dieter didn't know if this would be a reconciliation for them or further put a wedge between their relationship. He didn't want to fight with Greta, and he knew he'd done nothing wrong. But she obviously thought differently. Now he hoped she wasn't coming just to attack him, or try to discredit his work.

Emilia chuckled. "It will be fine. I'll run interference between you two, as long as you behave."

"Why wouldn't I behave? I have nothing against Greta, other than the fact she dislikes me," Dieter said.

"According to Greta, you stole her notes and wrote your paper and had it published quickly so she got no credit for all of her work." Emilia paused. "Be honest… is that what happened?"

"No, no, not really. That's not what happened. It's complicated," Dieter said.

"It's a simple yes or no. Did you steal her work and publish it as your own?" Emilia asked.

"Not exactly," Dieter said, feeling uncomfortable.

Emilia groaned. "It's true. You stole it from her."

Dieter's mouth was dry and he couldn't form words in his mind at the moment.

CHAPTER SIX

His contacts in the Polish government were not going to be helpful. Hans Koch was out of options, and might need to put his own boots on the ground and figure out where this search team was going to be headed.

If it was in the Owl Mountains, he felt like they might be able to stumble upon where the train was hidden. Not that he knew the exact location. His grandfather had made it perfectly clear it was never to be disturbed, that a great evil lived under that mountain and the dead should remain buried.

All very cryptic, but Hans knew his grandfather was right in one aspect of his thinking: it needed to remain buried so as not to drag the family name into the ground.

If the train and the treasure was found, the bodies would also be discovered. It would be traced back to Oberst Koch, who'd been in charge of the mission.

For now, it was only a legend. Nothing more than rumors and fantasy. Of course the world wanted to think the Nazi Party had stolen millions in coins, jewelry, gold, silver, precious artworks and more and hidden it all away under the mountains. They'd eventually come back and use the ill-gotten gains to start the Fourth Reich and take over the world.

That was always the legend of it all, the thought that kept men in fear and kept other men searching for their entire lives.

Hans knew it was really out there, somewhere, and he'd sworn to keep the secret safe. He'd told no one and knew his grandfather had never told another soul about it until his deathbed confession to Hans.

What is a good way to find out who is going to be leading a search? I have to find out, Hans thought.

He began calling everyone he knew, even people he hadn't seen in years or had only had a brief conversation with at some point. Asking them to keep an ear to the ground about an expedition in Poland in search of artifacts or anything related to World War II.

It made no sense to mention the gold train to anyone. He didn't want to get others excited about the prospect and have them also muddy the waters with their own search, and Hans knew everyone thought it was simply a good myth. A nice story about the evils of the Nazi Party from many, many years ago.

If anyone got an inkling it was remotely true, it could mean even more people looking for it. The odds were one small group would not be able to locate it, but if there were several teams wandering the wilderness looking, it could spell disaster.

Already, there was too much information in public. Hans had heard about it second- or third-hand but he didn't know where the rumor had first begun or who exactly was involved.

Of course, since he'd always tried to track this type of information online and in person, he had some clues as to the regular suspects, and knew Emilia Wagner's name kept floating to the top.

He'd actually met her once, at a function in Egypt years ago. She was a guest speaker about some rubbish archaeological thing. Talking about the cradle of life and the human race beginning in Africa but not where everyone thought it had happened.

Emilia's hypothesis had been shot down several times that weekend and she never actually wrote a paper on it, which was likely why her career hadn't ended before it started.

Not that she'd have been beaten up too much about it in the real world. Every crackpot floated some strange theory about aliens using our planet to grow pets, the flat earth nutcases screaming about their lost cause and another dozen that would make your head spin.

Hans only cared about preserving his grandfather's legacy. It was bad enough he was rumored to be a leader in the Nazi Party, although he'd wisely shielded himself from it all of his life. Still, Hans knew the truth.

His grandfather never had a guilty conscience for what he'd done to the inferior races. No, he prided himself on helping to eradicate some of them. Adler Koch only regretted blowing up the tunnel and sealing the fate of those men, thinking to his dying day there was something in the tunnel with them.

CHAPTER SEVEN

Because this operation was going to be so big, and involve a lot of money, Emilia had no choice but to ask her mentor, Roger Gladwell, if he could help.

Not that she wanted him involved, and she knew he'd want to come and be hands on with the expedition. She didn't want to be anywhere near him if possible, because if she were being honest… the man gave her the creeps.

Professor Gladwell had hit on her from the moment she'd first entered his class, but Emilia had made it quite clear she wasn't interested in easy grades by sleeping with her teacher.

Of course, he'd denied that was what he was trying to do, and had argued that if Emilia mistakenly brought this to the attention of anyone in the college he would deny and fight the accusation.

They'd come to a truce, where he kept his sexual innuendos and his hands in check and Emilia did her work and got something out of the class.

In the end, they had worked well together and Gladwell had become quite the mentor, helping her to achieve some of her dreams in the field.

There was always that lingering problem with Gladwell that Emilia never forgot about, though. She'd seen other girls come and go, all sucked in by the man's good looks and charm. Their careers were over before they even realized it, because the professor grew bored with them midway through a semester and then tossed them aside for the next pretty face.

Emilia had kept in touch with Gladwell and it had helped her open a few academic doors as well as get her some credit when she had articles published by some of the bigger magazines and online sites.

She waited until his class was letting out before entering the hall, giving him a wave.

Gladwell was talking to a young girl, likely his next conquest or the one on the way out, before he returned Emilia's wave.

"And what brings you here, my dear?" Gladwell couldn't help flashing his charming smile.

"I am in need of your help."

Gladwell shrugged. "Help? What exactly are you in need of from me?" He glanced at his watch.

"Sorry, do you have another class?"

Gladwell shook his head. "Tee time is in an hour. Playing with the dean as well as some bigwigs who think their idiot sons are going to be able to come to Harvard. Sad but true, the things I do for tenure."

"Then I'll make this quick. I need you to help me secure a private grant for something I'm searching for in Poland," Emilia said. She was hoping he wasn't going to ask a lot of questions, but knew he would.

"Poland, eh?" Gladwell rubbed the stubble on his chin, which Emilia knew he always had. He'd grow it to this length, so it looked like he didn't care about his looks. As if he was naturally attractive and didn't bother putting any more work into it.

"Yes. I need to hire workers, gather supplies, find suitable lodgings and on and on," Emilia said. She knew he knew the drill of what was needed for an expedition.

"I haven't been to Poland in years. I have a few colleagues there I'd love to see again." Gladwell grinned. "When do we leave?"

"Don't you want to know at least some cursory information?"

Gladwell shook his head. "If you're putting this together, I trust you and your instincts. I also know there is something important there and I'd like to see it, too."

Emilia didn't think he'd volunteer to accompany her. She was hoping he'd ask a million questions and she could deflect as many of them away as possible until he helped secure the money.

"Well, we're not going anywhere without a lot of money." Emilia opened her bag and handed the professor a stack of papers. "Here is everything we'll need."

Professor Gladwell smiled. "Is this a CIA document? You blocked out all of the pertinent information. Poland is the only location listed. It's a big country. Lots of archaeological items and sites to peruse. I might have a hard time taking money from someone if they don't understand what it is you're looking for."

Emilia shook her head. "I can't tell you anything more than what you have in your hand. If you can't do it, then I will have to find someone else. Thank you, sir."

She felt good not giving in, but knew he'd come back to her for more information and she'd have no choice but to give it over. There was no way anyone in their right mind would give her all that money without knowing what it is they were looking for.

Emilia could only keep planning and wait for an answer from Gladwell.

CHAPTER EIGHT

The initial answer came only two days later. Emilia had just gotten off the phone with Dieter, who seemed eager to get going. He had made a short list of like-minded individuals who would be perfect for this expedition, and most importantly could keep a secret.

When Gladwell called, Emilia was going over her notes for the hundredth time.

Gladwell was acting like it was no big deal; he'd actually gotten someone interested in the expedition, but they'd need more information and also a couple of spots for their own archaeologists.

Emilia didn't know how much she wanted to share and if it was a good idea to have added personnel on this journey, people she didn't know. Those types tended to want to make the key decisions since it was their money, and she knew they'd be butting heads.

"How much more information?" Emilia asked. She also wondered if they had really asked or if it was Gladwell wanting to know.

"A basic location. A region, even. What it is you're looking for would be nice but I told them there would be paperwork to sign so no info spilled out, and you were not likely to let them know until we arrived in Poland," Gladwell said.

"You're still going to come?" Emilia asked. Not that she thought he'd change his mind or be too busy for an adventure, but she had to ask.

"Of course. I'm also going to involve a couple of colleagues from the college as well as three who are currently in Poland I haven't seen in a long time." Gladwell paused. "If there is room for them. I think they could all be valuable to the mission. Whatever it is we're searching for."

"I can tell you the general area and that's all," Emilia said. She figured it couldn't hurt. There were more than enough legends and myths that had come from the area in the last couple of hundred years. "The Owl Mountains area."

Gladwell laughed. "Please tell me we're searching for the Wałbrzych Gold Train."

Emilia frowned, glad they weren't talking in person.

"I knew it. As soon as you said Poland I thought it had to be the Nazi legend." Gladwell laughed again. "Do you have some new leads and you think it is real?"

Emilia didn't know how to answer at first. If she admitted that was the target, could she trust Gladwell to keep it to himself, or would he have to tell the potential financial partner what they were looking for? If they knew this was about treasures and gold, would they want a piece of the action? Emilia wasn't interested in financial gain. She was more interested in seeing if the legend was real or not, and eventually repatriating the wealth back to the rightful owners.

She also wasn't naive enough to think other people wouldn't try to make this about the fabulous wealth they might actually find. While the Nazis had stripped everyone they'd conquered of their precious items, it would be hard to figure out who had what stolen. It might create an added wrench in all of this.

"I'll keep it to myself," Gladwell said. "Our little secret, but once we get to Poland you'll have to let everyone know what we're actually searching for."

"The area is vast," Emilia said.

"I've studied Project Riese at length in my younger days. Seven underground structures were built by the Nazis but none of them finished. There is still no idea what they were going to be used for. An underground base for troops, or to build weapons? Maybe secret weapons? A hideout for the Fuhrer, perhaps? Or were they going to store all of the treasure stripped from other countries? We'll never know." Gladwell sighed. "I imagine that area has already been gone over with a fine-tooth comb."

"But the Owl Mountains are over seventy square miles. Lots of valleys. If the theory holds, they had train tracks running through it at some point. Used it to drive a train filled with treasure and hide it," Emilia said.

Gladwell was silent for a few seconds. "We'll need to ask for more money, because we'll need ground-penetrating radar as well."

"Yes, I think we will. Drones to overlook the area and see if there are clues like sunken tunnels that have collapsed in the last eighty years, too." Emilia had all of her notes but she needed to figure out the logistics of a lot more things.

"Tomorrow, come to my office and we'll brainstorm a bit. I need to make a few phone calls. This is exciting," Gladwell said.

CHAPTER NINE

Greta knew better than to trust Dieter, so she was going to hedge her bets and bring in a couple of colleagues loyal to her. They both knew his reputation and what he was capable of, which would let Greta be at ease. If they had her back she could do her work and maybe gain some knowledge.

She might also become rich in the process. While publicly she was an advocate for history and learning about our past and all that drivel, she really wanted the big score. The pot of gold at the end of the rainbow, the financial security she so richly deserved.

Not that Emilia would know that. She was still so foolish when it came to history and archaeology. Emilia had the romantic notion they were doing great work, and the world would be amazed.

Greta wanted a pocketful of gold and silver coins to sell on the secondary market and live the rest of her life in comfort. After what had happened with Dieter, she knew never to trust anyone again. That included Emilia.

While Emilia seemed nice enough, normal enough, she could be hiding her greed well. Waiting for the big score herself. Greta didn't want to miss out. While the accolades to finding this great hidden treasure was also going to be wonderful, the real reason to tag along was for the payout.

Dieter was not going to get in her way, either.

Greta called Emilia and gave the names of her two colleagues who would be joining the expedition.

"Richard Smithson and Timothy Carter?" Emilia chuckled. "I know Rich and Tim. I worked with both of them a couple of years ago in Nigeria and Vietnam after that. Great men to work with. I'll add them to the growing list."

Greta didn't want to hear about a growing list. "How many more are on that list now?" She was trying to act casual with the question but heard the annoyance in her voice and hoped Emilia hadn't picked up on it.

"Too many, but I suppose it's needed. Do you know Professor Roger Gladwell?"

Greta frowned. "I've heard the name. The reputation. I think we're both too old for his tastes."

Emilia chuckled. "Yes, then you do know him. He's harmless but he brings with him the money part to this, but also an extra few eyes with it."

"What does Dieter bring?" Greta asked. She hoped she'd masked her annoyance in her words.

"He said he has a couple of colleagues he'll be inviting, archaeologists who know their way around Europe. So far he hasn't given me their names, so I can do some quick research on them. It's always nice to know who you'll be working with and if there are any personality clashes. With a couple of dozen people together, the hope is everyone gets along famously and we find what we're looking for."

"Hopefully there isn't a bigger clash than Dieter and I," Greta said.

There was a pause on the line. "I hope the two of you–"

"I'm fine. Just venting before I have to see him again," Greta interrupted. "You'll see. I am a professional."

I also want to get rich and never have to see Dieter or anyone else for that matter, Greta thought. "As long as he doesn't try to apologize or be my buddy, as if nothing happened, we'll be fine. A good working relationship is all I ask for."

"And that you will get. I promise. I will make sure he stays away from you except when absolutely necessary," Emilia said.

Greta frowned. "Did he say anything to you about my paper? His paper?"

Another pause on the line, which meant he had. He'd likely confided with Emilia that he'd stolen some of her work.

"I've got another call coming in. We'll catch up again soon, before we leave. Let me know what else you'll need from me. Bye, Emilia." Greta disconnected the call.

She didn't want to think about Dieter anymore, and it didn't matter if he admitted or denied what he'd done.

All Greta wanted to think about was how she was going to spend the rest of her life as a millionaire.

CHAPTER TEN

They arrived on his doorstep a couple of days before Dieter was supposed to fly out to Poland. Not unexpected but this early was a bit much.

"Can I help you?" Dieter asked, trying to block his door from the two men entering.

They were bigger and stronger than Dieter, and simply moved him to the side and entered.

Both men wore suits and sunglasses, even though it had been raining for the past three days. They walked throughout the apartment, as if searching for hidden gunmen or the police.

Dieter knew who they were and that Mister Moody had sent them, but he didn't want them running roughshod over his life.

"How am I going to explain to the others when I arrive in Poland with you two, huh?" Dieter asked.

"That's your problem, not ours." The man sat down on the couch and Dieter feared he was going to break it. "I'm Vincent and he's Scooch."

"Scooch? Is that a name?" Dieter asked.

"No dumber than being named Dieter, which is spelled like you're on a diet. Amiright?" Scooch asked and sat down on the comfy chair Dieter always sat in to read. "You got any Coke?"

"No, I don't do drugs," Dieter said, appalled. This was getting worse by the second.

Both thugs laughed. "Soda, you jerk," Vincent said and chuckled, pointing at his partner. "I called him a soda jerk."

"I get it. Funny." Scooch was staring at Dieter. "Coca Cola."

"I might have a can of Pepsi," Dieter said.

Scooch shook his head. "I didn't ask for Pepsi. I asked for Coke. Completely different soda. If I ask for Dr. Pepper, are you going to offer me Mountain Dew?"

Dieter shrugged. He wasn't sure. He'd never thought about or had to deal with beverage etiquette.

"What do you have to drink?" Vincent asked.

"Let me check." Dieter rushed to the kitchen, glad he had a break from their stares for a few minutes. "Not much. Bottled water. Milk. A couple of local IPA beers."

"What kind of bottled water?" Scooch asked.

"Spring water?"

Vincent groaned. "What kind, meaning Dasani, Fiji–"

"Fiji, yes, I get it," Dieter said.

"Bring us two of them."

Dieter frowned. He only had two left, but he wasn't going to argue with these very big men. He'd need to walk down to the corner store and purchase a few more before they left.

He'd also need to eat anything perishable in the next two days as well. "I'm going to make steak for dinner. I have an extra one if you'd like to split it."

Both men groaned.

"We're vegan, so you won't be cooking steak near us. We'll get dinner. Mister Moody gave us food per diem.

We're only going to be eating what God wants us to eat," Scooch said.

Dieter smiled, handing them both water. Neither of them thanked him. "What if God wanted us to eat meat?"

Vincent was up off of the couch so fast, Dieter stumbled back and fell to the floor.

"God wants you to stop killing his creatures, you imbecile," Vincent shouted.

Dieter hoped the neighbors weren't home, because they might call the authorities.

Scooch got up and went into the kitchen. Dieter stayed on the floor as Vincent sat back down after adjusting his suit jacket.

Dieter heard Scooch banging around in the kitchen for a few minutes. He came into the living room with a garbage bag. "I'm throwing all of this poison and death away. Where's the dumpster?"

Dieter sighed. "To the left once you get to the parking lot."

CHAPTER ELEVEN

Emilia was happy Professor Gladwell didn't try anything stupid while they were together, because she'd have to walk away from him and his money.

He wasn't a perfect gentleman, slipping a few inappropriate comments into the conversation, but it seemed to Emilia it was more a reflex than anything else. He'd been a scumbag for so long he didn't even realize how his words looked to her.

They'd met in a cafe a few blocks from her apartment, so that she wasn't alone with him and he didn't know exactly where she lived. She knew he was harmless, but why take a chance.

Not wanting to put herself in danger if there was even a small chance, she made sure she'd arrived early and was seated with her coffee when he appeared.

Gladwell went in for a hug but she stayed in her seat and put out her hand and they shook. "Can I get you anything? I see you already have coffee? I prefer tea."

"I'm good." Emilia took a sip of coffee and watched as he got in line.

Am I making the right choice? If he tries anything with anyone else in the group, will I be held responsible? I'll feel like it was my fault for bringing him in, she thought.

While she pondered this, she noticed Gladwell was busy not only ordering his tea but flirting with the young girl behind the counter who could be no more than twenty. The man was more than twice her age.

Emilia sighed. She needed to tell him not to be so damn creepy when they got to Poland, but knew she didn't have the guts to say anything.

"Ha, nice girl at the counter, thinking about options for college in the fall," Gladwell said with a grin. "I gave her my card and told her to message if she needed any help with anything."

You gave her your information because you're going to try to sleep with her, Emilia thought.

"I've secured more than the funding you requested," Gladwell said with another grin as he took a sip of his tea. "You're welcome."

"How did you manage that?" Emilia asked. She thought the first order of business was going to be a back and forth about more info needed before any money would come their way. This was a very good and positive thing.

Gladwell shrugged. "I had to give them a bit of information but don't worry. They don't want anyone knowing what is going to happen, so they'll keep it in-house and quiet. All we have to do is allow six of their workers to come along for the ride, help out a bit and see firsthand what we find."

Emilia frowned. "I hope you explained to them this was a scientific expedition and not about making money by selling the treasure we find."

Gladwell waved his hand dismissively. "Yes, of course, they get it."

Emilia doubted they did. She worried if they actually found the Nazi train and it was filled with everything she imagined, the money people would want to cash it all in and get their money back and then some. This didn't bode well for what she hoped to accomplish.

"I don't want too many cooks in the kitchen," Emilia said. "This could all get very confusing, whether we actually find it or not. I need those people to know there is a huge chance we will never find anything."

Gladwell nodded. "Trust me. They get it."

"I hope so." Emilia took a sip of her coffee. "This might take us several weeks, and I don't need the added stress of people thinking it will take a few days to find. Again… it might never be found."

Gladwell was staring at a young woman's rear end as she passed their table. "I have nothing but faith in your skills, Emilia. I know if anyone can find this treasure it will be you."

Emilia hoped he was right.

CHAPTER TWELVE

Hans smiled. He'd figured it out, and it had only taken him half of his life savings and a couple of future favors he'd need to give out when asked.

Emilia Wagner was her name, a woman who seemed to be on the edge of all of this. She'd had a few papers published, she was known but not well-known, and she had been looking for funding for her excursion.

An excursion to the Owl Mountains, which meant she had a general idea of where the treasure train was buried. Which meant she was getting too close for comfort.

Hans had figured out who was giving in their money and bought in himself, so their monetary loss wouldn't be as bad as initially thought. Angel investors they were sometimes called, and they liked the publicity in the end but not the financial hit.

He'd helped them to see he wasn't in this for fame and even fortune, but only for the history of it. Two things they didn't really care about. They might be into the fame part but mostly into the power to have money to throw away if need be. These types were gamblers who were too snotty to go to the casino or find a big-hand poker game in Beverly Hills.

The excitement was giving their money to a cause, one they didn't necessarily believe in, and see what happened.

Hans didn't understand it, but he was glad his money was now not only in with their money, but he was going as one of their representatives for the mission.

Now he could see firsthand if they'd find anything. He might be able to distract Emilia and her team to look in the wrong spots, too. Not that he knew the exact location but he might be able to find a clue on his own and then hide it.

Anything to keep them away from the buried treasure and what my grandfather did, Hans thought. If he could force them in the wrong direction, perhaps it would all fall apart and the harsh weather would come early enough to shut them down. The hope was that the following year Emilia would be unable to gather any more funds and have to stop looking.

They might have a two or three week window to find the collapsed tunnel, which would be a ridiculously short amount of time to search.

Even with the latest technology, Hans doubted they'd find anything important.

From what he gathered talking to his grandfather and doing his own research, there wouldn't be tell-tale signs. Adler hadn't painted symbols on the cliffs or put up a sign leading to the buried treasure. There were no maps detailing where it was, either.

The goal had always been to bury it in a specific spot that only his grandfather knew, and when the time came to give up the coordinates to the new leaders of the new Nazi Party, he was going to do it.

As far as Hans knew, he'd never been asked. There had never been another organized group that could do much more than seethe and talk about it, all growing old in their farmhouses in Brazil and South America, scattered, weak and all talk.

Hans needed to get ready. He had a meeting with Emilia and a few of the others in Wrocław to begin the preproduction of the journey. He'd been to the city before, once as a child, with his parents. They'd visited distant relatives, Germans who had been instrumental during World War II in keeping the Polish citizens in check. The actual details had been lost to time, and his family wasn't ever going to talk about what they'd done back then.

He knew they were proud of their accomplishments and had agreed with the teachings and solutions of the Nazi Party, which Hans had always found repugnant. Exterminating people for the color of their skin, for their religious beliefs, because they didn't have Aryan blood flowing through their veins was disgusting.

Suitcase packed and ready to go, Hans decided to cook some sausages and pepper with onions before heading to the airport. His goal was to get to Poland early and get a feel for the area on his own, before he had to smile and play nice with Emilia and her team.

CHAPTER THIRTEEN

Emilia was wondering whether or not she'd made a big mistake. This was all too much for her to put together on her own, and she didn't know who to trust to help with any of it.

While Dieter was her good friend and colleague, he was the first to tell you he was more creative than book smart, which was odd considering the jobs they had.

Professor Gladwell was too worried about his libido to be worried about spreadsheets and supplies and having enough bottled water in the remote mountain range.

Greta might be a good second, but Emilia felt like she was only along for the ride because she wanted to have her revenge on Dieter.

Then there was the newest member of the team, added at the eleventh hour, right before Emilia was going to fly to Poland.

Hans Koch, who had come highly recommended. He wasn't an archaeologist, per se. He was a definite fan of history, especially when it came to World War II and the Polish countryside. He'd studied in many places, all over the world, and had a team of laborers at his disposal, which would come in handy.

He'd even offered to meet with Emilia before she agreed to let him join the expedition. Uncalled for in this day and age. People like him usually begged and pulled in favors to be included, so they could bask in the glory of the finds.

Hans seemed… different to Emilia. More reserved. Confident in his abilities but not in an egotistical, arrogant way. He was sure of his skills and his weaknesses, and what he could bring to the expedition.

They'd met in a small cafe and he'd been charming. She put his age at a few years younger than her, maybe on the cusp of thirty at the most. He dressed well but not showy. There were no flashy rings, no chains around his neck, and she was glad he didn't have his ear pierced like Professor Gladwell.

"I've hiked the Owl Mountains," Hans said with a smile. "So beautiful, especially this time of year. Of course, there aren't a lot of good trails and not a lot of time before the first snowfall. And once it snows, it seems to never stop. The locals say the first snowflake will be followed by a billion more within the hour, so if we're out there we need to be prepared. Ever been to Florida?"

Emilia shook her head.

"Same weather, only with hot rain and not cold snow. Except in Florida it pours buckets, cats and dogs as they say, for a solid hour and then the sun comes out, dries it all up, and there is an intense humidity that drops like a dome." Hans laughed and shook his head. "Actually, hearing me say this analogy out loud to another person… it makes no sense. Poland and Florida weather is nothing alike. Forget I said it and don't hold it against me when you make your decision whether to have me or not."

Emilia had laughed. “Your resume is interesting. I’m hoping you can not only bring knowledge and a workforce but skills we might need. My only concern–”

“My experience in the field. I understand.” Hans shrugged. “What was your first dig, Miss Wagner?”

Emilia thought back to those wonderful times. “I was involved with a search for Raptha, the ancient trading port of the Roman Empire. Somewhere near Tanzania and Mafia Island. We found hints but nothing solid.”

Hans grinned. “That sounds interesting. Someone gave you a chance, right? All I want is a chance to see if this rumor is true or not. It is personal for me, too. My grandparents were swept up in the Nazi propaganda. I lost many relatives in Poland and beyond to what happened in World War II. I’d like to see the people, the families, get their rightful property back and help make restitution to them.”

Emilia reached across the table and shook his hand. “Welcome to the team.”

CHAPTER FOURTEEN

Dieter was glad to see the two goons who'd been shadowing him weren't seated anywhere near him on the airplane. One was a few rows ahead and the other, the one they called Scooch, in the last row of the plane.

At least I can relax on the flight and not have to deal with them, Dieter thought.

He made sure he didn't miss the drink cart when it went by, and he got into a paperback he'd brought along with him, about a repo crew in Florida who were going against a Colombian drug cartel. Dieter enjoyed exciting adventure stories, and knew he wasn't built for any of it.

The most he'd ever had to physically do was when he journeyed to Australia a few years ago with a team, to find lost tribes of indigenous people in the middle of nowhere. They never found the tribes, but he had a couple of nights of roughing it. Only a super tent and a cot with a few blankets, although Dieter did have a portable fridge on a generator so he had milk for his coffee in the mornings.

He worried he was going to disappoint Emilia by bringing these two thugs with him. He had no clue what these goons were capable of, but based on the time he'd spent with them… nothing good.

Vincent was the more refined of the pair, if you could even call it that. Like trying to say which restaurant had the more sophisticated burger, McDonalds or Burger King. At least Vincent ate with utensils.

Dieter had been repulsed by Scooch, who'd eaten fried rice with his fingers last night because he was too lazy to get up off of the couch and get a fork or even a spoon.

The men followed him everywhere, even though his apartment was small. His only privacy was in the bathroom, and they'd taken the lock off of the door so he couldn't lock himself inside.

As if I'm going anywhere, Dieter thought. He knew Mister Moody was gambling on Dieter and the team finding vast riches, and Mister Moody was going to get his fair cut.

Dieter worried he'd want a lot more of it, though. Even though Vincent and Scooch didn't have weapons on them, he imagined both were more than capable of hurting you with their bare hands. He also imagined they'd done it many times in the past.

Emilia is going to kill me if she finds out why these two are really with me, he thought. He asked for another alcoholic drink but was denied. They were going to land in Poland in less than half an hour.

Dieter took a deep breath. He needed to relax and enjoy as much of this as he could, all things considered. He'd been worrying about Greta Hagar in the beginning, but now that he had his two giant shadows, he hadn't thought of her until right now.

Greta might also kill me, and it will have nothing to do with the goons, he thought. She knew the truth and she was still upset, which wasn't surprising to Dieter.

While he had done the bulk of the work on his own, Greta's notes had helped him fill in a few of the blanks. He hadn't stolen all of it, but he knew he'd used enough to get her angry.

If he'd been called out and his work thrown in the trash, Dieter supposed he would've fought it to keep his name intact, but he'd known the truth.

Why hadn't Greta made more of a fuss about it? To this day, Dieter wasn't sure.

He hoped Greta would be civil and professional while they had to work together, but he wasn't holding out much hope.

Maybe I can apologize to her, Dieter thought. *See if I can make amends. Promise to write a paper with her and give her most, if not all, of the credit.*

When the plane landed Dieter wasn't surprised to see Vincent waiting for him, with Scooch pushing people aside and coming up from behind.

"Make the most of this," Dieter said under his breath, and went in search of his luggage.

CHAPTER FIFTEEN

Emilia had secured all of the rooms at a tiny hotel on the outskirts of Kolce, a small village. It was close enough to the spots in the Owl Mountains she thought they'd be venturing but far enough away from prying eyes.

That was the hope, anyway.

She knew the staff would ask questions, so she'd already concocted a cover story: they were a group of friends in the area to do some sightseeing at the Rise Project, the tunnels the Nazi Party had cut out of the mountains for storage, for defense and to build airplane parts for the war effort.

Now it was a tourist trap, and Emilia had actually been to it years ago. Luckily she spoke enough Polish to understand the tour guides, since the tour wasn't in English.

Before meeting for dinner in the main room of the hotel, she decided to freshen up a bit. Standing at the sink splashing water on her face usually calmed her down, but she knew her hands were still shaking. Was it her nerves, thinking she couldn't truly pull this off, or was there something else to it?

Emilia didn't know most of the people on this expedition. Could she trust all of them?

Any of them? That is a bigger question, she thought.

There was a knock at her door and she hurriedly wiped the water from her face, wondering who it was. She had no makeup on and was dressed in casual traveling clothes, which meant sweatshirt and sweatpants.

"Who is it?" Emilia asked at the door. She'd keep it closed if she could help it.

"Dieter. Let me in."

He'd seen her without makeup a few times. They'd been friends long enough and taken care of one another during the bad times, like sickness, hangovers and illicit drug stupidities.

Not that Emilia had ever done any hard drugs. A few tokes of marijuana had gotten her sick and Dieter had been there when her stomach had roiled.

He rushed inside and locked the door behind him. "I wish they'd leave me alone for five minutes."

"Who?" Emilia asked.

Dieter frowned. "Who? Uh, no one. The people I brought along with me. I'm not their babysitter. They need to get a hobby. Go and follow someone else around like puppy dogs. I just need a break for a few minutes. How are you holding up so far?"

"Great," Emilia lied.

"That's a lie. This is going to be good for both of us. Maybe even all of us. A vast fortune awaits," Dieter said.

Now it was Emilia's turn to frown. "This isn't about the money. I hope you know that. I hope everyone knows that. We're here for the history of it, and to hopefully return the looted family heirlooms and treasures to their rightful owners. Don't you agree?"

Dieter nodded slowly. "Yes… it's just… the people that had been robbed are no longer even alive. It would take a miracle to get their property back to their families, and who even knows who owned what. Right? I just think, and hear me out–"

"No. Absolutely not. I guess I'll need to nip this in the bud as soon as we meet for dinner. I know you're not the only one who has riches in mind, but that's not why we're here." Emilia was fuming. She wasn't even that mad at Dieter specifically, because she knew he wouldn't be the only one. "Time for dinner. Let me get dressed. I'll see you downstairs."

CHAPTER SIXTEEN

Emilia felt better once she'd begun the first dinner with the large group by explaining exactly why they were here and what they planned on doing once the treasure was found.

They'd all signed paperwork to that effect, but she still wanted to remind them.

After a couple of shots of bourbon, Emilia was thinking this might actually work without a hiccup.

As if that ever happens, she thought. She didn't know most of the faces in the room but each of them had been recommended by someone she did know personally, so that went a long way for her to feel comfortable with the group.

Quite a few of them, especially the men, thanked her for the chance to be on this expedition. Whether or not they were sincere was another matter, but she didn't care. At least they were here and hopefully they'd do what needed to be done.

When did I get so negative? This is a good thing, Emilia thought.

Dieter had given her a wave but hadn't approached her during or after the dinner, preferring to stay at the other side of the room and talk to the two men he'd brought with him. Whatever they were talking about it didn't seem like a friendly conversation to Emilia.

She stood and tapped a butter knife against her wine glass, getting everyone's attention.

When all eyes turned to her and conversation had stopped, Emilia smiled. "I want to personally thank each and every one of you for taking the time from your busy schedules to be here. This will be a monumental expedition. It will hopefully right a few wrongs from the dark past, and give back to those families that lost valuable family heirlooms. We're not here for the monetary value, we're here for the archaeological history of it all."

Everyone clapped but most did so because others were.

Am I a fool to believe they're here for the same reasons I am? They see dollar signs. This might not be good, Emilia thought.

She kept up her smile.

"Tomorrow we'll begin the scanning portion of the mountains. I have a worksheet I've put together, so various crews will be assigned in the event something anomalous is found underneath our feet and we can begin to excavate and work." Emilia made sure to add a dramatic pause now. "We only have a few short weeks to complete this, and the fear is the locals and the archaeological community will try to follow us, try to see what we're doing and what we're finding, and… we need to be vigilant. We need to keep quiet, our heads down and not give out any clues about what we've found."

"That's supposing we find anything more than a lot of dirt and rocks," Roger Gladwell said with a smile.

Emilia returned his smile. At first she thought Roger was being a jerk but realized he was helping her to not get anyone too excited about the possibilities. They needed to be real and focused. She knew there was something down there, somewhere, and she knew they would find it.

Greta was staring at Emilia, as if she were hanging on every word.

Emilia raised her glass. “I salute all of us who are here and doing this great work. For history.”

“For history,” everyone said and raised their glass in the air.

Now, if only every person in this room believed it the way I do, Emilia thought. She finished her drink and kept smiling, even though her stomach was roiling.

CHAPTER SEVENTEEN

The man was pointing down and smiling. "We have another void beneath our feet," he said in broken English. "Big one, too."

Emilia smiled, although she knew better than to get her hopes up. The last three voids they'd found were natural. The mountain range was covered in trees, mostly spruce, and it was slow going to even get the equipment to a patch of relatively flat ground to scan.

Add in a tunnel system they'd found yesterday that led nowhere, a remnant of the Germans boring through the mountain, and Emilia felt like she'd go home at the end of their time empty-handed.

Don't overthink this, she thought. "Keep going. I'm sure you'll find a few." She turned to Dieter, who was standing with the two men he'd brought with him. "Pass the word. Another void. We need to dig."

"How far down?" Dieter asked. He was sweating, even with a cool breeze blowing and trees blocking the direct sunlight.

"Not far. Get a team together." She glanced up at the bit of sky she could see. "We might only have time for one more dig, so let's make the most of it."

Dieter nodded and walked off to grab a few shovelers as well as the mini-digger they'd brought along.

Emilia noticed the two men were a step behind Dieter, and had been since they'd all arrived.

She knew she'd need to talk to her friend, if she could get him in private, and have him tell her the truth. These men weren't doing much more than shadowing Dieter. They were worthless to the expedition so far.

The team searching the ground was already moving along, lost in the trees. Emilia followed their trail to catch up. She didn't want to miss anything. She had to admit this was exciting, and every time they found a void underneath their feet she silently prayed this was the right spot.

During her research, she'd narrowed it down to a specific area of the Owl Mountain range, knowing they didn't have enough time to cover more ground.

It is either here or it is not, Emilia thought. With the tenuous grasp on the funding, she knew they'd likely not get another year to search for it. Now or never.

"Excuse me, miss. A quick word?"

Emilia turned to see Hans and a few others, all carrying shovels.

Hans smiled. "There are enough people digging back there. Mind if we walk with you for a bit? Stretch the legs. Maybe there will be another spot for us to dig, and we'll all be ready."

"Of course." Emilia smiled. "Every second counts, right? Even with three teams roaming the mountain, we have too much ground to cover. This is like finding a needle in a haystack."

"Yes, I agree." Hans wiped his face with a handkerchief. "Please, ma'am… lead the way."

Emilia turned and caught up with the team using the equipment and within fifteen minutes they'd found another spot to search.

Without a word, Hans began digging. The group with him dove in as well, and Emilia was glad at least some on this expedition were happy to dive right in and get their hands dirty.

Emilia felt inspired, and took a shovel from a man who seemed exhausted, and began digging herself. Maybe she'd get lucky and break into the tunnel with the train.

After ten feet and a lot of sweat, Hans put his hands up. "Natural pocket. No tunnel and no treasure. Next." He winked at Emilia. "This is more fun than I thought it would be."

Emilia winked back and had to agree.

CHAPTER EIGHTEEN

Greta knew she needed to stop drinking, because she was maybe half a glass of warm beer before she walked across the room and smacked Dieter in the face.

The bastard had stared at her whenever he thought she wasn't paying attention, and had tried today to actually speak to her, as if nothing had happened between them.

Greta had ignored Dieter, hissing under her breath to get away from her. Now.

She downed the rest of her beer and took a few steps in his direction, but Roger Gladwell intercepted her, taking her by the elbow and moving her to another corner.

"Get your hand off of me," Greta said, turning her anger toward Gladwell, who merely smiled.

"We need to talk, Greta. I don't believe we've ever had the pleasure, have we?"

Greta snorted. "Several times in the past. Don't you remember hitting on me, or any other female within striking distance? No thank you." She looked down at his hand. "If you don't let me go right now I will break your fingers. Is that understood?"

Gladwell shook his head. "No, I don't think we've ever met."

"Then your reputation precedes you. Unhand me."

"My bad. I apologize for being so… personal space is sacred, is it not?" Gladwell asked with a smile.

She didn't have time for this idiot. She rushed away, but Dieter was no longer in the room with the group. Where had he gone?

Greta knew she should let it go, especially in the mood and headspace she was in, but thinking about going another day with Dieter trying to mess with her was too much to take.

He is messing with me. He knows I can't do a thing about what he's done to me, and now he's here to rub my nose in it, Greta thought.

She went in search of Dieter.

He wasn't in the lobby, so she decided to barge into Dieter's room and confront him. Get it all out, once and for all. Let him have it and let him know to keep his distance during their work.

Greta got in the elevator and up to his floor. She started to step off when she heard an argument in the hallway nearby. She pushed the button to keep the door open and eavesdropped, because she thought she heard Dieter's voice.

"If you keep interfering, all bets are off," Dieter was saying to someone.

"Not even close, bub. Mister Moody owns you and whatever we get out of this little adventure will be a small part of what you already owe him. Got it?"

Greta knew it was one of the two men that had been following Dieter around since they arrived. Who was Mister Moody, though?

Likely Dieter has a gambling problem and he's into the mob for a lot of money, Greta thought.

Which meant he was here for his own selfish purposes, and now Greta worried it might mean trouble for all of them. What would these thugs do to get their hands on the treasure? It meant they were going to hurt people, and Dieter would only be the start.

Greta let the door close and knew she had to tell Emilia what was happening.

CHAPTER NINETEEN

Emilia wanted to cry. No way this was happening, especially to her friend Dieter. Especially now, when she felt they were so close to finding the train.

"What should I do? They haven't left his side," Emilia said. She hoped this was a mistake. Maybe Greta had misheard. She was obviously drunk, and she'd admitted she was looking for Dieter to confront him. Was she capable of being deceitful in order to harm Dieter, or to put a wedge between Emilia and Dieter?

Emilia felt a headache coming on.

"We need to separate them somehow and then one of us needs to talk to him and get the truth from his lying lips," Greta said.

Emilia waved her hand. "Let's put the past aside for now. This could have grave consequences for us today. Got it? Once we settle all of this, feel free to go after him. Until then… we need to think with clear heads. Who else can we bring into this?"

"No one," Greta said quickly. "If anyone else knows they might say something or do something and it might harm all of us. Who can you even trust at this point?"

Emilia didn't need this new problem. She was already so stressed with such a large group of people, most of whom she barely knew. She felt like she was on the edge of a cliff and about to fall off.

Get it together. Goodness. Don't overthink this and don't get worked up. This all might be nothing, Emilia thought. She knew she was fooling herself. "Then what can we do?"

"We wait. We watch. Keep Dieter and his cronies close at all times. Make sure they're with you starting tomorrow. They cannot be let out of your sight. I'll stick with you as well." Greta put a hand on Emilia's shoulder. "We got this. Just the two of us."

"Will that be enough?" Emilia asked.

"It will have to be." Greta smiled. "This is good because now we know what we're dealing with. Who we need to focus on and be wary of. I know this is a slap in the face and a big betrayal for you, since you and Dieter are so close. But long-term it will help you better deal with everyone around you. Right?" Greta hugged Emilia and patted her on the back.

Emilia felt awkward. While she and Greta were close, they'd never been physical. No hugs and kisses hello, nothing of the sort.

Am I now being played by Greta, too? It sure feels like it, Emilia thought. She truly couldn't trust anyone anymore, and it pained her to even think this way.

But Emilia knew it was true. "I need you by my side at all times, Greta. I'm worried."

"Of course, of course." Greta smiled. "Let me get you something to drink."

While Greta poured them both scotch, Emilia sat down in a chair and watched her friend. Were they actually friends, though? More like acquaintances. They knew each other because of the similar fields they worked in, because of other scholars and because they had an understanding about how things were supposed to work.

Emilia knew the only thing most, if not all, of the people on this expedition cared about was money and fame. A deeper understanding of history meant nothing to them.

They're all here for selfish reasons, she thought. *But... am I also here for the wrong reasons? It feels like it right now.*

CHAPTER TWENTY

Errol loved his job, but he loved money more. He knew this group was searching for lost or hidden gold, even though they didn't speak of it.

"We're archaeologists in search of videos in the mountain so we can study history," Emilia, the main woman, had said to Errol and his team when they'd first arrived.

All lies. He'd not been invited to their meals but he'd sat at the bar just outside the room where they met and had heard enough words leaking through the doors to know it had something to do with the Nazis and stolen items.

His family had been destroyed here in Poland because of the Third Reich. Because the Germans had decided Polish Jews were beneath them, not civilized enough to live.

Errol had lost all of his grandparents, and his parents had lived in fear all of their lives. Until the day they'd both passed away, quietly in their sleep within six months of one another, they waited for the SS to pound on their door and drag them away.

Were any of his own family valuables hidden away, maybe even here in the Owl Mountains? Doubtful. He knew they were poor and had nothing the Nazis would want except to eradicate them.

That didn't mean Errol wasn't going to get whatever he could because his family had been affected. He knew what a breach this would be, if he stole even a single gold coin.

But I earned it with my family blood, Errol thought.

He made sure to get ahead of the archaeologists as he scanned the mountainous terrain, wheeling his ground-penetrating radar quickly. He'd told his second, Merrill, to run interference whenever possible by asking a lot of questions if anyone from the group approached.

Merrill had worked with Errol long enough to know better than to ask questions, but he also knew there might be a decent payday ahead of them if they played it right.

"Here's one. Put one of our flags on it," Errol said, pointing behind him as he kept moving.

Merrill did as he was told, placing a small metal tab next to a tree root, so it looked like discarded trash. Maybe the top of a soda can. He had a pocketful of them, and so far he'd been able to leave four in their wake.

They were working in the area that Errol considered hills. Nothing too high up the mountain. He knew there were three other teams working in the higher altitudes.

Not only was Errol searching for voids, but he was searching for hits on gold, too. Then they'd get serious, not tell anyone, and come back at night and do their own digging, depending on how deep it was.

His plan was simple: they'd find the gold, come back and dig it up, and then the next day act like someone had likely followed them and dug in a spot they hadn't searched yet. Easy enough.

Erroll knew better than to grab the loot and abandon the dig sites. Then it would be obvious he'd had a hand in taking the treasure. No, he'd still do the job if they needed him.

Merrill trudged along behind him. The man was loyal to a fault. Depending on how much treasure Erroll found, he might even cut his partner in for a small share.

Not half. Nothing even close, but enough to keep the simple man happy. This could be the big score they'd been searching for all these years.

Erroll smiled when his scanner picked up not only a void underneath his feet, but a better sound: metal, likely gold, in the void.

"I think we found it," Erroll said. "And I think we're rich."

CHAPTER TWENTY-ONE

Greta was sick of sweating. Even when she found shade under a tree, it was still stiflingly hot. Wasn't Poland supposed to be cooler this time of year?

It was unseasonably warm. That's what that jerk Dieter had said this morning during a quick breakfast. Now she wished she'd stopped to drink more juice and take extra bottled water with her.

Richard Smithson and Timothy Carter were in step with her, and she wished they'd wander off and give her some space. They seemed to always get between her and whatever light breeze was blowing.

Emilia had already gone out by the time everyone began to wake and eat. Greta wondered where she was at the moment. They still had nearly ten days left on the mountain before the colder weather would move in, but it was so hot right now Greta doubted there'd be an actual winter.

"I think I see Emilia and a large part of the group up ahead," Timothy said and pointed.

It was definitely Emilia and they were on the ridge to the north and below where Greta was.

"Great. Even lower means even less wind and more heat," Greta groaned, more to herself than her companions.

It took them nearly half an hour to meet up with the others.

Emilia was smiling. "Greta, we've been trying to reach you on the radio."

Greta realized she'd forgotten to take her radio with her this morning. "What happened?"

"We found a hole," Emilia said.

"Someone dug it, though… looks like it drops into a void," Roger Gladwell said. He shook his head. "Either someone from our group or someone following us."

Greta knelt down near the edge. The dirt still had some moisture to it, which meant it had been turned over within the last ten hours or so. "Yes, I believe you're right. Is anyone missing?"

Emilia looked worried. "I'm not sure. Instead of holding a brief morning meeting I decided to get a jump and get right to work. I don't know if everyone is accounted for. We have several surveying teams spread out. I don't remember seeing any of them this morning."

"Then we need to radio each team and see who is missing." Roger got close to the edge of the hole and nearly tripped. He reached down and found a thick rope buried in the dirt. He traced it back twenty yards to a large tree, where it was tied to. "I'd say whoever did this is still below. Maybe. Or they found whatever they were looking for and decided to leave the rope, since they are long gone. Either way… this does not bode well."

Greta now saw the rope dangling in the darkness below. "How far down do you think it goes?"

"There's only one way to find out." It was Dieter, standing too close to Greta. For a second she thought he was going to bump into her and knock her into the abyss below. She crawled backward and stood near Emilia.

“I’ll need some volunteers to go down,” Emilia said.

Dieter raised his hand and the two goons with him both groaned and raised their hands.

“Then the three of you will go down,” Emilia said. She glanced at Greta. “Anyone else?”

Hans stepped forward. “I’ll be the fourth.”

“Then let’s get some tethers and whatever climbing equipment we have and get down there,” Emilia said. “I’m going, too.”

CHAPTER TWENTY-TWO

Merrill didn't think he was as stupid as Erroll thought he was. He'd kept his mouth shut all this time, all the years of working with Erroll, but he'd paid attention.

Recorded all of it, too. He'd go home at night and pull out his microcassette recorder and speak into it, detailing all of the illegal things he'd been forced to do by Erroll. All of the things they'd stolen, big and small, and how Erroll hardly ever shared the money once items were fenced and sold off.

Merrill wasn't going down with Erroll. Not a chance. He'd do whatever it took to not go to prison for the crimes, and there had been many over the years.

He was sure this was going to rival all of them, though. Erroll had been so excited when they'd been hired as one of the teams for this expedition, and he'd started planning where they'd spend the money even before they'd left home. Not that he even knew what the treasure might be, but he figured it would be huge.

"It's down here, I can feel it," Erroll said, shining his flashlight in Merrill's eyes.

"Where? You said you got a hit on metal but I don't see anything."

Erroll laughed. "Because, as usual, you're not looking with all of your senses." He kicked dirt on the ground and uncovered shining metal. "See?"

Merrill bent down and wiped it with his hand. It was a metal train track buried in the dirt. He stood and shone his flashlight in both directions. The tunnel was massive and his light just caught the ceiling in spots. "What is this?"

"Have you ever heard of the Nazi treasure train? I think we found it," Erroll said.

Merrill looked in both directions with his flashlight again. "Funny but I don't see any trains."

Errol kicked at the dirt. "Where there's tracks there's a train, stupid."

Merrill bit his tongue. This wasn't the right place to go back to Erroll. He glanced back the way they'd come. "Are you sure we're not lost?"

"How can we be lost? We came down the rope and walked down the tunnel. Do you remember any turns? Going into a side passage? No, because we didn't do anything but walk straight."

"Yes, but it feels like hours since we've been down here," Merrill said. He shone his light on the wall nearby and shuddered. Were they claw marks he saw in the rocks? "I don't like this. Maybe we should tell the nice lady who runs this what we've found. We can split the treasure with them since we found it."

Erroll scoffed. He swung his arms wide and spun slowly. "What treasure? I don't see anything, do you? No, because we haven't found it yet. Keep moving. At this rate we'll never get back to the rope and out of the void before the rest of them come to investigate. With our luck they'll find it right away and go in the opposite direction and get rich, while we wander for hours."

Merrill shook his head and started to walk, knowing the sooner they found it the better. “What happens if we find it, but then when we try to go back up the rope, that lady is there?”

Erroll shook his head. “Then we do what we have to do.”

“Hey, I didn’t sign up to kill anyone,” Merrill said.

“Neither did I, but sometimes you have to do what you have to do. Come on. We’ll worry about that once we find what we came down here to find, okay?”

Merrill could only follow. They walked for maybe a quarter of a mile more before Merrill heard something behind them, an echo of a footfall.

He turned and shone his flashlight, thinking he saw something but then again it was likely just a shadow.

“We need to go back,” Merrill said.

“Not a chance. We’re getting closer. I can feel it. Keep moving.”

Merrill turned and saw Erroll was strolling quickly away, so he ran to catch up, knowing in his gut this was a huge mistake.

CHAPTER TWENTY-THREE

Greta wanted to head down as well, but it was already too late to volunteer. She was glaring at Dieter, wondering what his game was, but the wimp refused to look in her direction.

Roger Gladwell came up beside her and smiled, pulling out a smoking pipe.

He thinks he needs to use that ancient thing because he's a professor, Greta thought. *He is a walking cliche.*

"This is some business, huh? Maybe we'll get lucky and the treasure train is underfoot." Roger lit his pipe and blew smoke rings into the air. "Did I ever tell you about the time, in Alexandria, when–"

"You never told me anything because I don't really know you, nor do I care to get to know you, old man," Greta said and walked away. She usually wasn't this rude, but right now she didn't want to hear one of his lame stories, trying to impress her. She knew who Roger Gladwell really was, and she wanted no part of his game.

"Are you sure about this? You're more valuable up here," Greta said to Emilia, who was standing near the edge waiting for the proper equipment.

Greta glanced over at Dieter and the two men that shadowed him. "Can you trust them? Can you trust him?"

"Yes, of course I can," Emilia said quickly. "I'll need you to coordinate from up here. We'll be in constant radio contact, okay?"

Greta nodded. "I can go in your place."

"I wouldn't hear of it," Emilia said. "This is exciting. I'll be careful. I want to see if this is the right spot."

"A one in a million chance this is actually where it is. Better to be up here and safe, rather than down in a hole. There could be gas trapped. Natural pits you could fall into. Underground rivers or falling rocks or a number of other pitfalls," Greta said.

"I want to go." Emilia looked like a child at the moment, being told she couldn't have any ice cream after not eating her dinner.

"We are all better served if you stay on the surface and monitor the progress," Greta said. She knew she was being selfish, and playing into Emilia's leadership, especially in front of everyone, was a low blow but she couldn't help it. She felt compelled to be the one to go down and find the treasure.

She glanced at Dieter, who still refused to look at her.

If I have my way, I'll be the first to see and touch the treasure. Dieter and his goons might get hurt in the meantime, because he deserves it, Greta thought.

She was scaring herself with these dark thoughts, even if they were about her enemy, Dieter. He didn't deserve to be here to see the treasure, to be a part of something so good and pure. Something that would change history.

Greta felt like Dieter would somehow steal it away from her, like he'd done before. He'd make this about him and Greta would be the forgotten piece of the puzzle. Again.

She wondered what the angle the other member of their descending party was, Hans. He was quiet. Too quiet. Maybe he was also scheming about the treasure, which was why he'd volunteered to go down into the hole.

I'll need to watch Hans. Keep him in front of me at all times, like Dieter and his thugs, Greta thought.

The ropes and gear arrived a few minutes later, and Greta made sure she was ready before any of the others. "Time to make history," she said to Emilia, who looked like she was going to cry for not going down into the void.

CHAPTER TWENTY-FOUR

Erroll stopped and turned back to Merrill. “Stop making so much noise.”

“It’s not me.” Merrill was looking back the way they’d come, shining his light back and forth. “I think we’re being followed.”

“By who?” Erroll stepped in front of Merrill but he didn’t see anyone. “Who’s there? Speak up.”

There was no sound in the tunnel. He looked up at the high ceiling but there was nothing above their heads but rock and dirt.

“Maybe it’s Emilia,” Merrill said.

Erroll turned and shone the light right in Merrill’s eyes. “Who is Emilia?”

“The woman who hired us.”

Erroll shrugged and turned back. “If it is, she’ll catch up soon enough.”

“How will we explain why we’re down here?”

Erroll shook his head. “We won’t have to. Things are going exactly as I planned. We’ll find another exit from these tunnels and move the treasure that way. Simple enough.”

Merrill didn’t see how that was much of a plan. An exit? Maybe this tunnel system had been sealed, like the legend said. Hidden away for a long time. Never to be found… until now.

"What if there isn't another way out, and we have to return to the opening we created? They'll be up there, waiting for us," Merrill said.

"And we'll tell them the truth: the tunnel was empty. A natural formation. Might even be noxious gas down here, very dangerous." Erroll was walking faster now.

Merrill turned and looked behind them, sure he'd heard something approaching. He didn't see anything but shadows.

Looking down as they walked, Merrill could see the metal train tracks and rotting wood. This part of the tunnel hadn't been covered by dirt, and he imagined it hadn't changed much in the many years since this was constructed.

Maybe there will be a train filled with precious items at the end of the line, Merrill thought.

They were following the train tracks, Erroll to the left of it and now Merrill to the right.

Up ahead was nothing but darkness. Merrill was starting to fear this tunnel would go on for miles and miles, and then suddenly dead-end into a wall of rock.

What if there had been a train down here, but it had been taken by the Nazis or some locals fifty years ago? It was likely because the legend had persisted for so many decades.

Maybe there never was a Nazi gold train. It was a rumor that had been started to give the lonely locals something to hang their hat on, so to speak. They wanted to have their own urban legends and their own part of the story.

This is a waste of our time, and then we'll have to explain to Emilia why we came down here and what we've been doing, Merrill thought. *We'll be fired. Maybe even arrested. We'll have nothing to show for it, either.*

"Woah," Erroll said, dragging Merrill back to the present.

Fifty feet down the track sat a dust-covered part of a train.

CHAPTER TWENTY-FIVE

Dieter turned to Greta as soon as they were down in the tunnel. "Look, for what it's worth… I'm sorry. I'll make it up to you. Tell me how to make this right."

"Your words aren't worth anything," Greta said. She glanced at the two goons standing behind Dieter. "If I don't accept your apology, are you going to sic your dogs on me? Is that it?"

"No, no, of course not." Dieter glanced over his shoulder at Vincent and Scooch, hoping they didn't get any stupid ideas. He knew the two were itching for something to break, looking for a conflict so they could fight. "Don't worry about them. Only I need to do that."

Greta frowned. "What have you gotten yourself into now?"

"Nothing I can't handle," Dieter said, knowing it was a lie. He leaned toward Greta. "They are bad people and they do bad things. Be wary."

"Is that a threat?" Greta asked.

Dieter waved his hands. "No. Of course not. I'm just saying… forget it."

The two goons walked up and Dieter thought they were discussing the best place to get a hot dog in the New York/New Jersey area.

"Can you two shut up for a minute? We have more important things to think about than hot dogs." Dieter shone his light both ways and saw they were in a pretty wide tunnel, and the ceiling was at least twenty feet over their heads.

"Rutt's Hut," Vincent said.

"Nope. Tommy's. Not even close." Scooch crossed his arms over his chest. "When we get back home I'm gonna prove it to you."

"Nothing to prove since you're wrong," Vincent said.

Greta stepped forward and hit both men with her light, right in the eyes. "Dieter said shut up. Now I'm telling you to shut up."

"I see something," Hans said, walking away from the group.

"Hey, don't go too far. We need to stay together." Dieter rushed to catch up with the man.

Hans was kneeling down and shining his flashlight on a train track, buried in the dirt and dust except for about a foot of it. "Whoever opened the hole and came down did this. Uncovered the tracks." He stood and shone his light ahead. "Are they dangerous? Should we have weapons?"

"Don't worry about that," Vincent said and chuckled. "We're well-armed."

Dieter, Greta and Hans turned to Vincent as he pulled a Glock from his waistband. "We came prepared."

"How'd you get them on the plane?" Dieter asked.

Scooch chuckled. "We have friends everywhere, buddy. These arrived the same day we did." He also had a Glock in hand. "I hope we don't have to use them. Time to stop chatting and find the treasure."

Greta groaned. "Is that why you're here, Dieter? You and your thugs are going to make off with the wealth?"

"No," Dieter said.

"Yes," both Vincent and Scooch said. They hadn't put the Glocks away. "Time to go find what we're looking for, ladies and gentlemen."

Greta glared at Dieter, who looked away, embarrassed.

Man, did I screw this up, he thought.

CHAPTER TWENTY-SIX

Emilia asked for another harness, but no one moved to do it.

"I need to get down there myself," Emilia said, pacing back and forth. "What if they need my help? They don't know what they're looking for. I do."

Roger stepped up and shook his head. "We need you up here, with us. The chances this is the exact hiding place for the train are one in a million, more than likely. There are other voids to check, and the radio just buzzed with another team finding another void not too far from here."

Emilia knew in her gut this was the right spot. "Then you lead a team over there and radio me to tell me if you find anything."

Roger shrugged and turned away. Emilia didn't know if he already knew what her answer would be or if he was disappointed in her.

Not that it mattered to her right now, because she had a job to do and that was finding the treasure.

Emilia paced around the hole, careful not to slide forward and to her death. *That would be something, right? So close to finding it and then I'm gone*, she thought.

As Roger took about half of the team with him, Emilia decided to sit and wait. The men that Greta had brought with her were off to the side, talking with anyone else who'd remained.

She knew she was setting a bad example by not working right now, but she needed to be close in case they found something.

When they found something.

"Can anyone hear me? How's it going?" Emilia asked into her walkie-talkie.

Static answered her, which was frustrating.

She repeated the questions but got no answer.

The group of people were now quiet and watching her.

"I need a harness," Emilia said.

No one moved to get her one.

Emilia knew she should stay where she was and coordinate from here, but she couldn't reach anyone below.

"What good am I doing if I can't be in contact with the team?" Emilia said, more to herself. She began pacing around the hole. "I need to get down there."

She knew she was standing on a slippery slope, and it was all in her head. When she'd first begun putting this expedition together, she had no idea how much she'd be wrapped up in it.

Her radio made a noise and Emilia stopped and lifted it to her face. "Hello? Can you hear me?"

If anyone was answering, she couldn't make sense of the fragments of words coming through. Emilia moved around the hole, hoping to get a better signal as she moved. Trying to find the perfect spot so she could talk to those below and hear their responses.

"Hello? Can you hear me? What do you see?"

Emilia went to the hole and dropped down to her knees.

"Hey, what are you doing? That's dangerous," someone said behind her but Emilia didn't care. She needed to figure out what was happening below.

Emilia lowered her head and shoulders into the hole, along with her hand holding the walkie-talkie.

"Hello? Can you hear me? Tell me what is happening," Emilia said.

CHAPTER TWENTY-SEVEN

The train was real. Erroll laughed and touched the dusty side of it to make sure.

It was the fabled train, the legend come to life.

"We're rich," Erroll said quietly, as if speaking the words loudly would shatter the train before him.

Merrill came up next to him and laughed. "We did it."

I did it. Not you. This was all me, Erroll thought. He wiped a tear from his eye.

"Where is the entrance? It looks boarded up," Merrill said as he began to walk around the box cars. By the light he could see there were at least a dozen of them connected to the train engine. All covered in dust and dirt.

Erroll could see the doors to the engine had been welded shut and the windows covered with steel sheets and also welded. The doors to the box cars were chained shut with several padlocks on each as well as metal welded shut.

He knew it would take some tools to open the doors and get to the valuables. The damn Nazi punks had made sure this wasn't going to be easy.

"Erroll… come and look at this," Merrill said from the other side of the box car.

At first, Erroll was going to ignore Merrill, and figure out how to get inside the box car, but there was no way he could do it with his bare hands. Maybe his buddy had found a trap door or an opening, so he walked around to the other side.

Merrill wasn't looking at the train, he was shining his flashlight a few feet away.

"What is it?" Erroll asked.

Merrill didn't need to answer because it was lit up as far as the eye could see.

Human remains. Bones. Shredded Nazi uniforms. Guns and ammo. Supplies.

Death.

"Like a killing field. A predator's spot to feast," Erroll said. He turned and shone his flashlight all around them, expecting to see a jaguar or a panther approaching.

As if reading his mind, Merrill asked a question. "What types of big predators are in these mountains?"

"I have no idea and I don't want to find out." Erroll thought there must be at least a dozen bodies strewn about in the dirt, and he wondered how many more they'd find if they kept looking.

Erroll decided to stop looking. He needed to get inside the train and get rich.

"I don't like this. Maybe we should leave and come back with the right tools to break into the box cars, and maybe more men so they can help us carry it all," Merrill said. "If every car is filled with treasure… there'll be more than enough to help us for the rest of our lives, no?"

Erroll didn't want to share it with anyone else, especially Merrill.

"We can maybe find another way out, too. If we go back the others might have already found the rope and the hole and we could get in big trouble." Merrill was slowly turning in a circle, watching around them. "I saw something before. I thought I did, anyway. I don't think we're alone down here. I think–"

Erroll turned in the direction his partner was looking when he heard Merrill's scream.

CHAPTER TWENTY-EIGHT

Vincent was annoyed. Annoyed he had to be here, in this godforsaken country, annoyed that he had to follow Dieter around, annoyed he was working with Scooch again, and annoyed in general.

He could be home right now, feet up with a cold beer in hand watching sports. It didn't matter the game, either: football, cricket, tennis, American football, even baseball would be better than this.

I swear, once this is over with, I'm going to lose some weight. Get on a good diet. Hire a personal trainer, a chick with a skinny butt I can stare at while doing pushups and situps and whatever else she'll have me do to torture me and get me to lose weight, Vincent thought.

He wanted to punch the Greta woman in the face right now, too, because she was annoying.

Vincent had no doubt Dieter had screwed her over somehow. He seemed like a weasel of a man, and he imagined the only way a guy like that could get as far as he'd gotten – which didn't seem too far to Vincent – was by taking advantage of other people.

Greta had been used and thrown away, but she wasn't a former girlfriend or love interest. Vincent could tell their relationship was platonic. The chick was cute and Dieter could never score a babe that hot.

Vincent could if he wanted to, but he was working. On the job romances were always a mess, especially if

Mister Moody decided he'd had enough of this and wanted Vincent and Scooch to clean house and kill them all.

"Enough with you two lovebirds fighting. We need to find out what's down here, and the quicker the better," Scooch said.

Vincent noticed the other guy, Hans, was busy walking around them in a circle and shining his flashlight to see what else was down here.

Not much but dirt so far.

"We follow the train tracks. This is a good sign," Hans said. He began walking before anyone could ask a question or comment.

"I guess we'll table this for later, but there will be a later," Greta said, shaking a finger at Dieter. "In the meantime, stay clear of me, you piece of garbage."

Vincent smiled when Dieter didn't respond, acting like a dog with his tail tucked between his legs.

If a woman talked to me like that, especially with other people around, I'd have to knock her down and show her who was boss, Vincent thought.

Scooch was already walking down the tracks, kicking at it with his shoes to clear the dust and dirt away.

"You can all stand around and argue. I'm going to get rich," Vincent said and turned toward Scooch.

"Rich? We're not keeping the treasure, you idiot," Greta said.

Vincent was used to acting and reacting before thinking. He turned and slapped Greta across the face, not hard because he wasn't close to her, but caught her enough to stun her. Put her on her butt in the dirt.

She looked like she was going to cry but then looked angry as she stood and dusted herself off. "Emilia will hear about this." Greta turned and looked at Dieter. "Shame for bringing such a hooligan with you."

Dieter stepped over to Vincent and jabbed a finger in his chest. "One more incident, one more word out of you, and guess what? I tell Mister Moody you tried to steal from him. You wanted the treasure to yourself and you were going to cut him out of it. Is that what you want?"

"Wait, wait… who is Mister Moody? Cut of the treasure? Dieter, what's going on?" Greta asked.

CHAPTER TWENTY-NINE

Emilia knew they'd only been down there for less than thirty minutes but she was too impatient.

Already, another crew on the mountain had radioed in that they'd found another void.

But this is the right one. I can feel it, Emilia thought. She turned to the group standing around with her and waved her hands. "Time to get back to work. I'll need three people to wait with me here, ready to go down if need be." She pointed at three people randomly. "The rest of you head to these coordinates. There is another void."

"Maybe it ties into this one," someone said.

"Yes, maybe. There's only one way to find out." Emilia didn't want to be a jerk but she knew they were wasting precious time. They had a finite amount of hours to hunt for the treasure, and her fear was that they wouldn't find it and when they finally got the funds and manpower to return next year, it would be too late.

She watched as most of the team walked off, likely annoyed with her attitude and her focus on this one hole.

I'm doing the right thing. I've found something and I need to fully explore it before I can move on, Emilia thought.

She knew that someone else had found it, either someone working with them or an outsider who'd been watching where they were looking.

If it was someone with her team, part of her team, there was no reason they hadn't reported this back. Unless they were hurt, but there was no person at the bottom of the void with a broken ankle or worse. No blood anyone had reported. Nothing but a tell-tale hole in the ground.

Which meant they were dealing with someone who was not aligned with what Emilia was after. These were fortune hunters, someone who wanted to take the treasure for themselves and get rich off of it, not show the world there could be some good coming out of the atrocities of World War II.

Emilia imagined the smiles from the families as heirlooms, long thought lost, reappeared.

"I need to get down there," Emilia said.

She was waiting for someone to tell her no, but the people remaining were trying to look busy with the gear. No one was looking at her, possibly afraid she'd go off on them.

"I need some gear," Emilia said loudly. She had no time to be nice because she felt like this was all slipping away from her.

What if the thieves found another exit from the mountain? While she was standing here doing nothing they might already be moving the treasure down the other side and heading home with it.

A couple of the remaining people glanced in Emilia's direction and she smiled and waved at them to help her. "I need to go down."

They helped her to get fixed up with the proper gear and stood by, waiting for Emilia to get lowered down into the hole.

“Do you want any of us to come with you?”

Emilia knew by the looks on their faces none of them wanted to follow her down. They were here for the discoveries but not to do the dirty work, which was fine.

She could do this on her own.

“Lower me down, please,” Emilia said as nicely as possible. Not that she thought anyone would do something mean or hurtful, but why take the chance when another person had your life in their hands. Literally.

She checked her flashlight and also had a knife strapped to her leg, hoping the supplies she had would be enough.

Hoping there was still treasure down there. Somewhere.

CHAPTER THIRTY

Merrill was confused. One second he'd been staring at Erroll and the train and the next he was face-first on the ground with a searing pain running up and down both of his legs.

He screamed at the pain and tried to turn over but there was something on his back, pressing him into the dirt.

The pain continued and Merrill saw Erroll take a step towards him but stop, as if he was in shock. Couldn't believe what he was seeing.

"What is it?" Merrill yelled. He tried again to roll over and managed to get onto his side, whatever was on his back now off.

As if everything would be better now.

"What the–" Merrill was stunned to see black creatures, maybe three feet tall, like little monkeys with long tails and huge teeth and claws, surrounding him.

They were taking turns ripping their claws against his legs and Merrill saw with horror they were shredded. His left leg's skin had been peeled back to the bone.

Erroll ran over and kicked at the creatures, but they danced away easily.

Merrill tried to get to his feet but he now saw his right foot had been sliced off, barely attached, dangling.

The pain was beyond reason and he screamed again when he saw what was left of his foot.

This is not happening. This is not happening, Merrill kept thinking over and over.

Erroll tried to grab one of the creatures but it darted away, and Merrill saw with horror as two of them jumped onto Erroll's back and began clawing at his neck and head.

"Get off of me," Erroll yelled, as if that would get them to stop.

Erroll stumbled past Merrill, tripping over what was left of his partner's foot and falling to the ground.

"We need to get out of here," Merrill said. He knew he was going to die. Even if these things stopped ripping them apart, he was going to bleed to death and soon.

Another creature swiped at Merrill, who put his hands up to block and lost a finger on each hand. He could only watch as blood pumped from this latest wound.

Erroll was fighting back, thrashing on the ground and punching at the little monsters, but they easily stayed clear of his swinging arms and kicking feet.

"We need to go," Merrill said. He didn't know what else to say, really. Admit they were going to die? Yell at Erroll for getting him into this mess?

Erroll finally connected with one of the creatures, slapping it a few feet away.

"Take that, you little–"

Before Erroll could finish his sentence, a dozen of the creatures struck him from all directions, high and low. They didn't fly but they seemed to be able to leap high.

It was impressive to Merrill, even if he knew there was no escape.

Merrill began shouting, as if anyone would be able to hear his cries.

No one knows we're down here. No one is on the way to rescue us. We are on our own and we are going to die, Merrill thought. "Thanks a lot, Erroll."

A creature stepped up close and slashed Merrill across the throat with a razor-sharp claw and Merrill felt himself fade to black.

CHAPTER THIRTY-ONE

Hans Koch held back, letting the rest of the group walk ahead. He didn't want to follow them because he thought they might be headed in the wrong direction.

Not that he knew. His grandfather hadn't been forthcoming about the location of the hidden tunnel or, once it was found, which direction to go.

The train tracks went in either direction and the group had assumed they were heading the right way based on Greta seeing some footprints.

Footprints made by whoever got down here ahead of us, not by those who gave their lives for the treasure, Hans thought.

He watched as they moved farther and farther away, no one bothering to see if everyone was still together. Hans turned off his light and stood still until they were far enough away he could turn in the opposite direction and search on his own.

When he turned on his flashlight he thought he saw something off to the right, but when he swung the light around there was nothing but the cavernous tunnel. Dirt and rock.

Taking a deep breath and blowing it out, he saw just how cold it was down here. Typical for underground voids but there was no breeze. Nothing stirred his breath, which meant this passage had been completely sealed until they'd broken through.

Even now, Hans watched as his breath rose slowly towards the ceiling and the entrance that had been broken in.

The tunnel was perhaps thirty meters from wall to wall and twice as high, with the train tracks running as far as he could see in either direction.

He followed the tracks, stopping every few feet to rub his boot to make sure it hadn't curved away. Not that he thought it would. This track had been put down to serve only one function: to get the train into the mountain and hidden away, not to be a track used to transport anything from one point to the next.

It was here for one purpose, and either Hans was going to stumble into the lost train or he'd hit a dead end and need to go back the other way.

Hans had nothing else to do, and so far he'd done the minimum on this expedition, staying out of the line of sight of Emilia and who he thought the main people were running the show.

His work was to observe and make sure no one found the train, but now it looked like it was inevitable. Hans hated to think about what he'd have to do to keep this secret a secret.

The tracks kept going in a straight line, which was nice and easy to follow. Every few meters he'd stop and make sure he was still on the same straight line of track.

Hans stopped when he heard something fall nearby. He swept the light all around but there was nothing to see. A fallen rock? There was nothing else in the tunnel that could fall.

Yet, he didn't see a rock. All he saw was solid rock that had been demolished many, many years ago, the marks still obvious in the walls.

Hans looked up to the ceiling and gasped because he swore he saw a shadow moving just out of his light's reach, a brief second of a creature or person up there.

Which made no sense because no one could be up there, and there could be no creatures living in the tunnel. Surely, he would have seen signs of them: droppings, nests, whatever food they could scavenge.

There can be nothing down here alive, Hans thought, but he knew with all of his heart and all of his fear that he was not alone.

CHAPTER THIRTY-TWO

Roger Gladwell stared at the man running the ground-penetrating radar unit. "And… what do you want me to do about it?"

The man shook his head. "I'm trying to reach Emilia but she's not answering. We need to make a decision. There's a tunnel underneath our feet, a long narrow void. Only a couple of meters down. If my estimates are correct, we're several kilometers from where they found the initial hole this morning. This could be the other end of it." He stepped three paces to his left and pointed at the ground. "Here? No void. Solid earth." The man shuffled back to his original position and pointed down again. "But right here? The beginning of a void that goes in that direction, right in line with–"

"Yes, yes, I get it. I'm not an idiot. Are you asking me to make an executive decision and set the shovel to dirt?" Gladwell was intrigued by what had been found, and despite there being several other workers in the immediate vicinity, the man had come to Gladwell as if he was the de facto leader here. "Then I say we dig."

It was easier to apologize than ask for permission. Gladwell was sure Emilia would let them dig, too, if she were reachable.

Something was unsettling about where she could be. Was it simply the mountain that was running interference on their signal? If he found the treasure he could take charge of the expedition and certainly be the lead for interviews about it. After all, he'd be the one to discover the treasure. Why shouldn't he be the most important person and the one they'd want to interview?

Not Emilia or the others, who weren't even here right now. What could they add to it, right? 'Oh, we were in another hole that led nowhere but Gladwell found the treasure so we eventually walked over and saw it' or some rubbish like that.

Gladwell wasn't going to dig but he waved at the others milling about to do it, firmly taking charge of the site now. "Be careful, it isn't that far down but it might be as deep or deeper than the void found a couple of hours ago, so please be careful."

At least a dozen people grabbed picks and shovels and began ripping up the harsh terrain, tossing shovelfuls of dirt out of the way.

"Should I keep looking?" the man with the equipment said to Gladwell.

"Yes, of course. See if it truly leads back to the other cave they found." Gladwell was hoping the man would walk off with his team, because he wasn't going to share this find with them. He'd tell the press he stumbled upon it himself, in fact. No one cared about the hired help and what they'd added to the expedition.

Within thirty minutes they'd opened up a sizable hole in the ground, and Gladwell took a couple of steps forward and smiled.

The bottom was no more than three meters down, a slope of rocks. He knelt and shined his flashlight into the hole and saw it drop gradually down, naturally, and into a deep tunnel not unlike the one the other team had had to get ropes for.

"I'm going down," Gladwell said. He knew if he let anyone else go before him, they would be the first to see the Nazi gold train and then they might get all of the glory.

Gladwell wasn't going to have any of that, so he began shouting orders, letting everyone know he was heading down by himself at first to assess the dangers. Then everyone else could join him, once he knew it was clear.

Once I see the train, Roger Gladwell thought.

CHAPTER THIRTY-THREE

Erroll turned and blindly ran, not knowing or caring which direction he was headed. All he knew was he had to get away, because small furry monsters were busy ripping Merrill apart.

He got maybe ten meters away, running next to the train cars, when he saw a gap between them and decided he'd never be able to outdistance the monsters. Maybe he could find a hiding place and eventually someone would be down to save him.

The sounds of Merrill being torn apart made Erroll want to vomit, and he closed his eyes for a second and leaned against the train, forcing himself not to puke.

He heard noises in the box car he was pressed against and knew he had to hide, but he was curious what the noise was. There was a rusty set of beams ascending the box car, and Erroll decided he might be able to climb up to the top and hide.

One step at a time, his weight pressing on the metal. He thought he'd break one of them off but they held.

He got to the top and saw this box car had an open top. Afraid shining his light would attract the creatures, he shone it down for a brief second.

That was all Erroll needed.

He turned his head and puked.

Inside the box car was a swarm of fat, white rats. Hundreds, maybe thousands of them. All squirming about.

What the hell? Was that what the creatures fed on when human flesh wasn't available? I need to escape, Erroll thought.

He took a closer look and saw cockroaches as well, millions of them. Erroll flinched when a cockroach crawled near his hand, and he released his grip and fell back to the ground, barely staying on his feet.

Erroll didn't know where to go now. He ducked down and shined his light quickly under the train and saw despite all of the dirt built up there was a gap he might be able to fit into.

Dropping down to his hands and knees, Erroll turned off the light and hoped he remembered the way in the pitch black of the tunnel.

He heard scraping noises all around and knew it wasn't just the rats and the cockroaches. It was the creatures and they were surrounding him.

Erroll crawled as fast as he could and thought he was in the clear until he felt a terrible pain in his left ankle, as if someone had shoved a hot coal into his exposed skin.

The burning sensation grew and he realized due to the pressure, one or more of the creatures had gotten a hold of his foot.

Erroll tried to turn over onto his back so he could kick at them, but they now had his other foot pinned to the ground.

Both of his legs were being ripped apart, either by claw or teeth. It was hard to tell and the monsters were relentless.

Erroll heard a cacophony of noise and realized a second later it was coming from his own throat. He was screaming in pain, in anguish and in fear.

Now they were pulling him out from under the train and he wondered how long before he'd pass out or they'd kill him.

He lost track of time but it felt like hours before they'd ripped apart his legs up to his waist, stripping the flesh from his bones.

Erroll finally passed out but not before his throat had gone hoarse from all the yelling.

CHAPTER THIRTY-FOUR

"Did you hear that?" Greta asked the group. She frowned. "Hey, where's that other guy?"

"Which guy?" Dieter asked.

Greta waved her hand. "The quiet guy. Hank or Han or something or other."

"Hans," Vincent said. "I think he went the other way."

"What? Why didn't you stop him or tell us?" Greta asked.

Vincent shrugged. "Who cares where that little creep goes. If he finds the treasure he's done all of the hard work for us. If he doesn't and he went the wrong way, he'll be killed or lost. No great loss, if you ask me. He was weird, even by this group's standards."

Greta groaned but she didn't say anything to the man. If she were being honest, she was scared of him and his partner. These were men who would break your leg over a small gambling debt. They might even be capable of killing someone and then going to lunch.

She saw that Dieter was also staring at Vincent but not saying a word.

I need to speak with Emilia once this is over. Before the treasure is found, actually, because these goons might start killing everyone who stands in their way of riches. Whoever Mister Moody is surely sent them with Dieter, Greta thought.

Greta wondered what part Dieter played in all of this. Was he in cahoots with the pair, or had he been roped into this somehow? Drugs or gambling debts, perhaps?

Emilia was going to be devastated to find out Dieter was definitely part of a bigger conspiracy. While the women had talked about it previously, there was no real proof. After what Vincent had just said, Greta had all the proof she needed to let Emilia know and for them to do something about it.

But what, exactly? It wasn't like they were going to apologize and walk away if Emilia asked them to. They knew what was at stake. Not historically but definitely financially.

"We need to keep moving," Greta said. She pointed in the direction they were headed. "Dieter, after you."

"Yes, of course." Dieter glanced at Vincent. "Mind going ahead and leading the way? Not sure what else could be down here."

Vincent looked like he was going to argue but then Scooch shrugged and started walking. "See if you ladies can keep up. If I get to the train first it's mine."

Greta didn't know if the man was joking. She didn't think he was. Could they be walking to their death? It seemed likely but she didn't know what else to do. Head back to the hole and the rope and get help?

There was no help from above. All she could do was keep the thugs in front of her at all times and see if Dieter was on their side or would also be killed.

Greta felt all alone down here. She was jumpy, too, and kept shining her light all around. Expecting something to come out of the darkness and attack her.

"How far do you think we gotta walk?" Scooch asked. "My feet are killing me already. This ground ain't even, either."

Greta was about to tell him to shut up, knowing he could snap and kill her with his beefy bare hands, when everyone stopped.

There had been a blood-curdling scream from up ahead.

"Is that Hans?" Dieter asked.

Greta knew it wasn't. "He's somewhere behind us now. Whoever came down ahead of us. More than likely."

"More than likely they ran into some trouble," Vincent said.

More screams echoed throughout the tunnel from up ahead.

CHAPTER THIRTY-FIVE

Hans found the end of the line and it didn't stop at a train car filled with stolen treasure.

It ended at a pileup of rocks and dirt and he knew he'd found the original entrance. The train tracks led right into the jumble of boulders.

This is where my grandfather blew up the side of the mountain and condemned men to die with the treasure, Hans thought.

He turned back the way he'd come and shined his light, as if now he'd be able to clearly see the train. Nothing but darkness.

Hans wondered how far the tunnel ran. He'd imagined only a few meters, enough to fit a train engine and perhaps a few boxcars into it. If his estimation was correct, he'd walked nearly eight hundred meters already, and that was just this part of the tunnel system. It could go a lot longer down the other end. He wasn't sure if they'd dropped down in the middle of it, either.

The Nazi diggers could have tunneled for kilometers into the mountain before they'd been satisfied it was deep enough no one would be able to find what they were hiding.

Plus, Hans knew they had prisoners of war doing all of the hard work, and there were no breaks or stoppages unless someone fell over and died.

He didn't want anyone to see any of this. It was an embarrassment to his country, to his family and to the world.

Better to let it all lie forever and eventually it will all go away, Hans thought.

It was a fool's way of thinking and Hans knew it. Eventually all of these awful things were dragged into the light and ripped apart. The world would know what his grandfather had done, especially if they found the bodies of the prisoners and soldiers alike.

And why wouldn't they? None of them had ever escaped. Hans knew there had been Polish soldiers and locals scouring the Owl Mountains in the days after the train was hidden, but no one was ever found. No bodies, no one escaping the tunnels.

Hans didn't want to be around when they found the stolen items and the dead.

The idea of coming with Emilia and her team had been simple: to make sure no one found what they were looking for. To watch and see if anything was found.

Hans was sure they were in the right place. The train tracks were the obvious giveaway.

It was only a matter of time before it was all put together.

This was not a good day for his family, or for those who let this atrocity happen to begin with.

The sins of our fathers, Hans thought.

He started the journey back to the rope, hoping Emilia would raise him back up. He'd give her an excuse about being separated from the group, about claustrophobia, about being frightened. Whatever it took to get him away. Then he'd rush back to the hotel, pack and be on the next flight out of the country.

Hans knew this was all going to blow up and he wanted as much distance from it as possible.

Shadows danced in front of his light and he swore more than once there was something small but solid just out of reach of the light.

He hoped it was his nerves and his eyes playing tricks on him.

CHAPTER THIRTY-SIX

Emilia didn't know which way to go at first. There were footprints in the dirt going in both directions, but when she squatted down to take a closer look she saw only one set had gone to the right and the rest to the left.

She followed the group of tracks to the left, noting the train track that the footprints seemed to be following.

Every now and then it looked like someone had scraped the train tracks with a boot to clear it of dirt and debris.

Emilia wondered how far the tunnel went and how far away the others were, and who had originally found the tunnel to begin with.

She was excited at the thought of finding the Nazi train and the items stolen all those years ago, and being able to get it out of the caverns and back to the proper owners.

Not that she had any idea how to make that happen. Not exactly. She'd done as much research as she could to know the right agencies to call when the treasure was found, but she worried they'd take it all and it would never get back to the families who originally lost it.

Of course, eighty-odd years later, the people who it had been stolen from were long gone. What would happen to items that no family lines remained, or no one knew who it had been stolen from originally? So many questions Emilia had no answer to, but that wasn't going to stop her from doing what was right.

Her real, immediate worry was that whoever had come down here in the middle of the night was up to no good. They might have already taken part or all of the treasure with them, which would not be good.

Emilia wondered if she'd have any recourse if items began to show up on the black market within a few weeks or months. What could she legally do? It wasn't like they'd stolen it from her. Not directly.

Not many people even knew about this expedition. If she tried to publicize it after the fact and the treasure was missing, it might show the thieves they needed to go even further underground with their selling of valuables. It would also make every item even more valuable, too.

There was no winning for Emilia unless she got her hands on the train and was able to secure it so no one could exploit what was inside.

She stopped and took a good look around. Nothing but rock and dirt and a train track running in both directions. She could see the tool marks and the blackened areas where they'd used dynamite to clear some of the rock.

With all of this work done, there had to be a train filled with loot down here. Had to be.

Emilia started walking again, wondering why she didn't hear echoing voices from up ahead. There was no sound and what little she heard was muffled. She'd been in caverns and caves many times in her life, but they usually threw sound back at you. Down here it was dampened. Weird.

Emilia hoped to run into the group soon because she was starting to feel lonely. She could only see to the end of the light and that wasn't really far.

Up ahead in the distance she thought she saw a light but it could just be her imagination.

They are down here somewhere. I just need to find them... and the train, Emilia thought.

CHAPTER THIRTY-SEVEN

Dieter was panicking. He was between a rock and a hard place right now, with nowhere to run. Nowhere to go and no one to help him.

And he knew he'd done it to himself.

His gambling had gotten the best of him, as well as his slippery slide down when it came to morals. Dieter knew he should have told Emilia what was happening. She was a friend, likely his only real friend, and yet he'd duped her into taking him and these two goons along, as if all was great in his world.

They're going to find the train and then shoot us, Dieter thought. He knew it for fact, too.

Dieter especially saw it in Vincent's eyes. He was the leader of the two, and Scooch would do whatever his partner said. Mister Moody had given them specific instructions on how to handle any scenario, and Dieter knew once the treasure was found the simplest plan was going to be the one they picked: kill everyone.

Greta glanced back at him a couple of times and she looked angrier now than when he'd stolen her notes.

Why am I such an awful person? I deserve all of this. I always seem to do the wrong thing and I make it worse by trying to get out of it. Like what I'm doing now, Dieter thought.

Vincent was staring at Dieter as they walked and his hand hovered near his gun tucked into the front of his pants.

I hope he stumbles and the gun goes off and shoots his family jewels, Dieter thought.

"So, hey, while we have time just walking in the dirt here… what's the story with you two?" Scooch asked, pointing at Dieter and then Greta, as if they didn't understand the question and who he was talking about.

Dieter glanced at Greta, hoping she wouldn't go off again about what a jerk he was. He knew he deserved it, but still… It hurt. He actually liked Greta. When he'd first met her he was going to ask Emilia about her dating situation and perhaps turn on the charm and see where it led, but he'd blown it.

"There is no story. Not really. My friend Emilia introduced us and he hit on me and then decided I wasn't going to date him so he stole my research and used it for his own work and then he got the fame and fortune and I got nothing," Greta said.

Dieter was glad she hadn't shouted her answer. In fact, she looked defeated. Her anger was replaced by frustration. That's how Dieter saw it. Maybe facing the fact it was done, it was in the past, and there was nothing that could change it now.

"I'm sorry–"

"Don't," Greta said with a bit more venom to her words now. "Don't talk to me. I've warned you already."

Scooch laughed. "Wow, you two are so in love with each other." He turned to Vincent and shrugged. "Can't you see it, too?"

“Oh, yeah, definitely. She’s kinda cute in a nerdy sorta way, but still out of his league,” Vincent said.

“Thanks.” Dieter didn’t know where to look right now. They’d all stopped walking.

He knew if he looked at Greta she’d likely go off on him again, which he did not want.

I deserve anything she says to me and more, he thought.

Dieter held his head up and looked directly at Greta. He was going to take it and say nothing back, because when he apologized she attacked again.

Greta shrugged her shoulders and stared at Dieter. “What’s done is done, right? Hopefully we have an understanding now and I know who you truly are. You also hopefully know who I truly am, and what I will do if you cross me again.”

Scooch laughed. “See, I told you. These two are in love. You’d better invite us to the wedding, because we saw it here first, right?”

Dieter hoped Scooch talking about an event in the future, however unlikely, meant he wasn’t planning on killing them down here in the dark abyss.

CHAPTER THIRTY-EIGHT

Hans leaned against a wall, suddenly overcome with vertigo. Was it the walls closing in on him, the still air, or the fear finally catching up and paralyzing his entire body?

He struggled to right his mind. Shaking his head, he pushed away from the wall, as if it was holding him back, as if it was his safety net he didn't need.

The shadows crept closer, seeming to taunt Hans.

"Leave me alone," Hans whispered, or maybe it was only in his head.

He felt the history of the Nazi treasure train like it was a solid mass, oppressive and pushing down on him.

As if his grandfather was standing in the tunnel with him and looking annoyed he'd turn against his family.

"I'm turning against what you did in your life, I'm trying to change the past so you don't destroy the present family. Don't you understand that, der opa? Even you were upset about what you've done, so don't look at me that way. I am only trying to right a wrong our family – you – committed. I cannot stand by idly while Emilia and her team uncover the horrors you've committed, whether you like it or not," Hans said.

His grandfather stared at him for a long minute before he faded away.

I'm losing my mind. He was not here. I need to get a grip on myself and focus on the task at hand, Hans thought.

He needed to get down to the other end of the tunnel, where the train had to be. By now someone had found it. If he was lucky it might be the two goons with Dieter, who would kill everyone else to keep it for themselves.

Hans knew it was an awful thing to wish for, but it might work out in his favor.

If these obvious mobsters had the treasure, they wouldn't be on the front covers of every magazine, the front page of every website, talking about it. No, they'd sneak it out of the country and no one would ever hear about it again.

The paintings would be sold on the black market and no one would know where they'd come from and the buyers wouldn't care. As for the gold and silver? Melted down and repurposed another way, or sold by weight. There might be tons of metal to liquidate.

Hans shook his head. There was also going to be so many other things like jewelry in the train, things he needed to see to believe.

By now they should have found the train, but he wasn't going to rush. It might be better to hide in the shadows near the ropes to see who eventually tried to exit.

Hans had a feeling it wasn't going to be everyone. There would be some double-crossing because people were greedy.

The hope was that he wasn't directly involved in any of that. If they found the treasure and they were civil about it, so be it. He'd try to push the narrative to the happiness of finding the treasures and not to how they got down into the mountain to begin with, or who was in charge of doing it.

No matter what, Hans needed to protect his family first.

He wondered just how far he would go to protect it, too. There might be some tough decisions ahead for him.

CHAPTER THIRTY-NINE

Emilia heard random noises, but she couldn't figure out where they were coming from. Above? Behind? In front of her? It was a lot of echoes and she chalked most of them up to dripping water or rocks moving.

Her imagination was running wild right now, and she needed to stay focused.

This had been a dumb move to come down here alone, and she wished someone else had had the guts to accompany her.

Emilia knew she should have stayed topside and coordinated from there, in the event they found the treasure. There was no way she'd find it first, so at the most she'd stumble upon them rejoicing at the find.

There was definitely something in the tunnel with her and she spun around but didn't see anyone or anything.

Of course there will be animals down here. This is their natural habitat. I'm the intruder, Emilia thought.

There had to be other entrances after all of this time. The air was stale but not like when she'd entered that recently discovered tomb outside of Egypt. You knew it hadn't been opened in a long time.

Emilia groaned. *You are an idiot. We never checked for gas or harmful chemicals in the air before we came down. What if I'm feeling weird and paranoid because my brain is being affected? Stupid, stupid.*

She thought about heading back up and finding the equipment to check but hesitated. What if they'd found the treasure already?

What if they died already, too? This will be on you, she thought.

Emilia decided to do the right thing, which was to make sure the tunnel was safe.

As she headed back toward the ropes she heard a scraping nearby. When she turned to the sound she saw what had to be fresh claw marks in the rock.

Deep, too. Low to the ground, likely an animal that walked on all fours and not that tall.

Emilia knew the animals that frequented this part of the world but she'd never done more research than a list of them. It didn't really matter, because a wild animal would attack if provoked or if it thought it was in danger.

She spun around but there was nothing nearby that could have made the claw marks. But she knew there was something here, and it might be stalking her.

Fearing for her life, she moved quickly, making sure she shone the light behind her every few feet so nothing was gaining at her back.

As she got back to the ropes and saw the shaft of light from above she smiled.

Hans Koch stepped out of the darkness from the other way and Emilia screamed.

"Just me. Have they found it yet?" Hans asked.

"I don't know. I was going topside to get some equipment. To check for the toxins in the air and–"

Hans shook his head. "No, I think everyone needs to stay down here. We have a lot of work to do. Let's take a walk, shall we?"

Emilia was about to protest until she saw the Glock Hans was pointing at her.

CHAPTER FORTY

"What's that stench?" Dieter asked.

"Who cares? I see the train," Vincent said. He laughed. "It does exist. I woulda bet good money it was just a legend. How 'bout that?"

As the group started getting closer, the smell was even stronger.

"Is that a body?" Greta asked, covering her mouth and nose.

Scooch chuckled. "It used to be a living person. Man, he got ripped apart." He leaned in closer. "Not even sure if it was a he or a she."

Dieter wanted to turn around and run. This was not a good scene. Whatever had happened to this person was going to happen to them. He was sure of it.

"Hey, I think I see another body near the train." Vincent was already walking, halfway to the train.

Dieter shook his head. "I'm done. I'm heading back."

Greta stared at him until she shook her head. "Too late for that. This is a crime scene. I'm going to call Emilia and let her know to call the authorities."

As soon as she pulled her phone from her pocket, Scooch smacked it away. "I don't think so, babe." He walked over and stomped on her phone, destroying it.

Greta looked like she was going to cry.

"It probably didn't work down here, anyway," Dieter said, trying to comfort her. If Greta lost it he knew he was out of luck. Not that he thought either of these goons were going to let them live.

"Yeah, this dude is in pretty bad shape, too." Vincent chuckled. "Hey, Scooch, remember the time we hung that guy over the railing at the Four Seasons and he slipped?"

Scooch laughed. He glanced at Greta and Dieter and shrugged. "It was cold out. Rainy. My hands weren't dry."

"This guy looks like that, like he fell six stories and hit the pavement. Real bad shape. I think his insides are missing, too, like something sliced him open and ate his organs," Vincent said.

"What could do that?" Scooch asked.

Dieter saw what could do it a second later, when a dark shape appeared on the roof of the train engine.

Greta saw it, too, because she shined her light up and the creature put its claws over its face before running away.

"What the heck was that?" Scooch asked.

"I don't want to stick around and find out," Dieter said, turning to run away.

His light showed him what was behind the group: dozens of the little monsters, only a couple of feet tall, covered in coarse black fur and with overlarge teeth and claws.

Your worst nightmare come true.

Vincent screamed and Dieter turned to see three of the creatures jump down and drive Vincent into the ground. Claws and teeth moved so quickly Dieter lost count over how many times the man was attacked.

Dieter joined Vincent with the screaming, long after the goon had stopped.

CHAPTER FORTY-ONE

Hans shook his head when he saw Emilia look up.

"If you scream I will not only shoot you but whoever looks down. I will kill every person on this expedition and you will be to blame, because you dragged us all out here," Hans said.

"Why are you doing this? Just take the treasure and go," Emilia said.

Hans shook his head. "No, you don't understand."

"Then explain it to me."

"Where to begin? Okay… my grandfather was a Nazi. Oberst Adler Koch," Hans said.

"I don't know that name."

Hans put up a finger. "Ahh, but if this treasure sees the light of day, you will. He was the one in charge of not only gathering all of the stolen money, jewelry and precious artworks, but also loading the trains and bringing it here. To this very spot. He made sure it was deep inside the mountain before closing it all up."

"So Hitler and his sick minions could retrieve it at a later date and use the funds to continue their attempt at world domination," Emilia said.

"Exactly. Except… he told me years later there was something inside the cave with his men and the prisoners assigned to the trains," Hans said. "Instead of rushing in and helping them he sealed them inside. Alive."

"Oh my God."

Hans nodded. "It haunted him throughout the rest of his life."

Emilia frowned. "And you want to keep the treasure hidden so his mistake, his cruelty, will never see the light of day."

"Yes, very much so."

"And does that mean you'll kill dozens of people to keep your family secret then?" Emilia asked.

"It means I need to take control of this situation. I don't want anyone else to die over this train, but… I have to protect my family more than anything." Hans didn't want to shoot Emilia or anyone else, but he knew he'd likely need to. There was no way he could let them go free. Not now. He'd drawn a gun at a defenseless woman. He'd have to do the same for anyone else now.

"We can work this out. No one has to know about your grandfather. Surely you see that." Emilia sighed. "We need this to be seen. For those that lost heirlooms in the past. They need them back. Paintings and rare items that need to go back to the museums they were looted from during World War II."

"No. It will come out, especially now that I told you," Hans said.

"I don't care about that part of history. No one will come after you or your family, even if it gets out. He did what he was ordered to do. Right or wrong. You could argue he didn't have a choice, he was forced, whatever spin you want to make on it." Emilia looked past Hans now. "I just want to find the treasure and let the world see it."

Hans stepped back and glanced over his shoulder, expecting Emilia to be bluffing so she could wrestle the gun from his hand.

Instead, he saw a nightmare rushing at him.

They both had their flashlights aimed at several small dark hairy creatures, who were trying to sneak up on them.

Hans turned and shot one in the face, dropping it to the ground, twitching. More appeared.

CHAPTER FORTY-TWO

At first, Emilia was focused on Hans and the terrible things he was saying. She thought he was going to kill her to hide his family secret.

Until she saw movement in the dark behind him and hoped it was Greta and Dieter heading back to the ropes to let them know they'd found the treasure.

Only it wasn't her friends. It was a nightmare come alive.

Hans turned and saw them, too. It wasn't her imagination running wild.

He fired and killed one of them but the rest kept moving forward. The craziest part was some of them were scaling the tunnel walls to get above them.

"They're up, too," Emilia shouted at Hans.

He looked up and fired two shots and two of the creatures fell to the floor, dead.

But Emilia knew he didn't have enough bullets to kill all of them.

"Help, help us!" Emilia started to shout, looking up the ropes, hoping someone was paying attention and had heard the shots. She knew there was no time to reattach herself to the ropes and climb up, especially since these monsters could climb very fast.

There were several monsters above her now, and at least two slipped up through the hole and disappeared.

Oh, no. We've let them out. They'll kill innocent people. They'll terrorize the countryside, Emilia thought. She knew she was losing her grip on reality now.

Emilia and Hans were surrounded. The creatures stayed back, likely fearing Hans' weapon, but Emilia knew at some point they would regain their courage and attack. In one deadly mass.

Hans turned and shot another one, killing it.

Emilia noticed the creatures on either side of the now-dead one dragged it back into the darkness.

"What will they do with it?" Emilia asked, as if the answer would mean anything, as if either her or Hans would ever know.

Hans ignored the question and shot another one. "We need to get up the ropes. Hook yourself and then me. Don't try to leave me down here, either. We need to escape."

Emilia grabbed the ropes and clipped her gear to it, but they needed someone topside to hoist them back up.

"Help, help, let us come up. We're in trouble," Emilia yelled. She clipped Hans and now they were side by side.

Emilia's screaming seemed to annoy the creatures, who started to take a step forward, chittering. The sound was awful.

Hans shot two more and the monsters retreated a couple of steps back.

"How much ammo do you have?" Emilia asked. She wondered if Greta and Dieter could hear the shooting from wherever they were in the tunnel, and if they'd come to investigate. Maybe putting them in danger of being attacked and killed.

"I don't have enough to kill them all," Hans said.

As another couple of creatures took a step forward on small hairy legs, Hans shot them.

He turned and fired again… and then the next pull of his weapon did nothing.

Hans was out of ammo and the creatures seemed to recognize this, because they all took another step forward.

Emilia looked up, hoping someone would rescue them.

CHAPTER FORTY-THREE

Scooch grabbed Greta by her arm, trying to swing her around so she was between the monsters and Scooch.

"Get off of me," Greta yelled and tried to get away from Scooch, who was holding on for dear life.

Dieter came to her rescue, punching Scooch in the jaw.

"Is that all you got?" Scooch asked, releasing Greta and punching Dieter in the face. Dieter went down hard.

Greta needed to get away but there was nowhere to go. The monsters were all around her and she looked up to see them on the walls and on the train and the boxcars.

Scooch had his hands up and was grinning down at Dieter, forgetting the creatures all around them.

Until two dropped from the ceiling above and drove Scooch to the ground. He rolled over, trying to pull them off of him, but Greta could see fangs and teeth sinking into the neck and arms of Scooch.

Greta's first instinct was to pull them off of Scooch and help the man, but she knew it would be no use. By the vacant look in his eyes as she used her flashlight to see his prone body, she knew he was already dead.

His neck had been sliced open and he was bleeding profusely. Even if that hadn't killed him, there were so many other wounds on his body already.

A few more creatures moved in and began slicing parts of Scooch up, while others were still doing the same to Vincent a few feet away.

Dieter stood and went to Greta, who gripped his arm tightly.

"We're going to die," Greta whispered, afraid to speak loudly in fear the monsters would remember they still had two victims that were alive.

"Back up slowly and then we run," Dieter said. He began moving. Even though there were creatures all around them, the group behind the pair seemed to move aside to let them pass.

They're going to let us live, Greta thought. *We're going to be good. They only wanted the two goons to eat. Only those two.*

They took a few more steps away and the monsters around them moved to join in on the fun of tearing Vincent and Scooch apart.

Greta gagged as she smelled the blood and saw the small monsters tearing strips of flesh and muscle from the bodies and eating them.

None of the creatures were looking in their direction.

"We can do this," Dieter whispered. "Don't make a sound."

"Then stop talking." Greta knew she was one look from those menacing eyes or a creature taking a step in their direction and she would lose it. Her body was shaking and her legs felt like rubber, but she kept moving back, keeping her eyes on the grisly scene. As if looking away might let them know she was trying to get away.

She'd heard stories over the years of colleagues, ones who got into the field and stumbled upon wild animals, who said they always kept eye contact.

You never looked away from a predator because then they'd attack, Greta thought.

Dieter turned away from the monsters and spun Greta around, too.

"Run," he said.

Greta got a couple of steps and heard a shriek behind her, knowing they'd done the worst possible thing.

CHAPTER FORTY-FOUR

The first thing Roger Gladwell saw was the outline of a boxcar in the distance and he picked up his pace, eager to see it with his own eyes. Stand beside it. Slide the doors open and see the vast wealth hidden inside for decades.

He'd followed a natural break between the rock formations until he'd stepped out into a tunnel that was clearly man-made.

Shining his flashlight on the ground, he saw where the train tracks ended only a few feet from the last boxcar in the line.

I wonder why there is no engine on this side, since the tracks go no further. Did they back in the train? That would be an odd thing to do, unless... Roger smiled. Of course. The intent was never to leave the train and its artifacts in the mountain, but to come back at a later date and drive the train out and use the items.

Roger didn't need to wonder what had gone wrong with the plan: The Third Reich had lost the war. Their leaders either killed, arrested or supposedly escaped to South America to live out the rest of their days under assumed names.

All of this loot was now for them to find. For him to find, in fact.

Roger thought he was the first to see the train and he smiled, but as he began walking and shining his light down the boxcars to the engine he paused.

There was blood on the ground. A lot of blood, in fact.

Another step forward and he saw the bones and they looked gnawed on, and they looked human.

Oh, no. There's a large predator down here, Roger thought. He spun around, looking for tell-tale signs or tracks.

His light only went so far but what he saw was unnerving. White eyes. Dozens of them. Just out of reach of his light. Sightless eyes.

Roger was initially excited because he might have stumbled upon a new species of cave-dwelling creature he could show the world.

They seemed to be blind and small.

A couple of them stepped into the beam of the light and Roger gasped. They were like nothing he'd ever seen before, and they didn't look friendly.

Claws and fangs. Dark hair.

Roger heard a noise above him on the boxcar and shined his light in that direction.

There were several on top and they looked poised to spring down upon him.

He turned to run and put some distance but only got a couple of steps before he was attacked, several of the creatures falling from above and driving him hard into the ground.

Roger tried to turn over and fight them off but he felt the claws and fangs sinking into his flesh. These creatures were the predator that had already taken out at least one person who'd gone down into the void.

His flashlight was knocked from his hand and extinguished, which was just as well.

Roger couldn't see his attackers anymore, but he could feel them as they slit into his skin and poked his eyes out with their sharp claws, slicing his neck from end to end in a final strike.

He faded to black.

CHAPTER FORTY-FIVE

"Go up the rope if you can. Save yourself," Hans said to Emilia. He was bleeding from his weapon hand, the Glock knocked away and kicked into the darkness by the creatures. "I'll try to hold them off as much as I can. The world needs to know what is happening down here."

Hans kicked out, catching one of the monsters in the chest and driving it back.

The rest of the group seemed to hesitate, not inching forward to strike.

Maybe they think I still have a weapon that can kill them. Maybe they're being cautious because they finally met a foe that can take them out, Hans thought.

He saw they were blind, so their hearing and other faculties must be sharp.

Hans began to scream loudly, hoping the noise would drive them back, but it only seemed to irritate them.

Emilia was heading up the ropes, which was fine. One of them had to live to tell this fantastic story, and Hans knew he'd never make it unless he was helped up from someone topside. It would be no use for him. He'd never gone up and down these guideline ropes before today, and had no clue how they actually worked. Coming down was easy enough but ascending would be confusing, and he knew the monsters could scale the walls and ceiling easily enough and cut him off.

Hans needed to make sure they paid attention to him and not Emilia right now.

"Come on, you little punks, and fight me," Hans yelled, spinning in place and waiting for one of them to approach so he could kick at them. Throw punches. Whatever it would take for them to keep their focus on him. "Emilia, if you can hear me, don't make a sound. They can't see us but they can hear. Sense vibrations, maybe. Be as calm as you can while you ascend."

Hans didn't know if she heard him or how far up she'd actually gone. His fear was that she'd be killed while climbing and she'd fall on top of him.

He moved off to one side, still throwing punches and kicks but the creatures were giving him plenty of space.

"Come on and face me," Hans said. He'd never been much of a fighter growing up but he thought he could hold his own in a fair fight. This, however, wasn't going to be a fair fight.

They were shifting all around him, as if they were setting Hans up.

Hans thought they likely were, and he knew he was going to die very soon.

Surprisingly, he'd made peace with it.

The sins of our fathers, he thought. He would pay the price for what his grandfather had done all those years ago, and the Koch family would end in the same spot where evil had occurred. Were these creatures the manifestation of what had happened? God's way of making sure no one could ever touch the treasure hidden in the tunnel?

Hans would be a willing sacrifice in order to keep order.

As soon as Emilia was safe. It was the least he could do, a heroic act to balance some small measure of respect. Perhaps in time Emilia would tell the story and what he'd done to save her from his likely fate.

"Come on and get me," Hans yelled and jumped forward, kicking a creature in the chest and dropping it to the ground. He smiled and lifted his boot to stomp its dark head into the ground.

Hans realized what a mistake he'd made too late.

Off-balance, they came at him from all angles. Striking him high and low in a coordinated attack.

He felt the claws scrape across his torso and felt the puncture of fangs into the side of his neck. They knew what they were doing because the pain was intense but only for a few seconds, before his neck began to spurt blood and Hans felt his life draining.

His eyes rolled into the back of his head and he stopped breathing, dragged to the ground.

CHAPTER FORTY-SIX

Emilia began climbing up the rope and it was a struggle. She'd only had to do this once or twice in her life, and only then because it was a challenge from another climber.

Being hoisted up would be ideal, but so far no one from above was looking down and her pleas for help had been ignored… or fell on deaf, dead ears.

When Hans had told her the creatures couldn't see but they could hear, she stifled the building scream inside and clamped her lips shut.

She kept moving up and up, feeling like she'd need to climb miles and miles up this rope, knowing she'd never make it.

Where was everyone? Were they all dead… because of her? She'd put this together, she'd invited everyone, she'd dragged them out to the Owl Mountains on a search for this train and this treasure.

Emilia wondered if there was even treasure down there. She hadn't seen any. There could be a train filled with stolen loot, or they'd opened a hole into Hell where these monsters resided, waiting to be freed.

She was breathing loudly and had to slow herself down, the panic getting the best of her.

Hans was down below screaming at the creatures, egging them on to fight him. He was sacrificing himself for Emilia and she wasn't really sure why. Minutes before he'd had a gun aimed at her chest, wanting to kill her and everyone who'd come here. All to protect his family's legacy.

Emilia found the strength to keep going, one hand over the other, feet and legs working in tandem to propel her body up.

She was close to the lip of the hole now. Still no one above she could see, no one to help her get out. It was all on her shoulders right now, and her shoulders were on fire from the strenuous climb.

I need a hot shower or a hot bath with bath salts, Emilia thought. Trying to stay positive, trying to think of a future where she was still alive.

What would she tell the media when this was all over? If she was able to escape the creatures might easily escape, too. They could terrorize the area and beyond. How many were there, too? The tunnel could be filled with hundreds of them.

In her mind she pictured a nightmare: dozens of these dark monsters roaming the countryside at night, killing everything in their path. If they reproduced at a decent rate, in time they could be everywhere.

Emilia would be the person who set them free, and she tried not to cry. Not right now. She'd have time if she got out to dwell on it. Self-loathing and self-pity were in her future.

She managed to get to the top and pulled herself out of the hole, expecting her legs to be grabbed at any second and tossed back down, her body breaking on the hard ground.

Instead, she was out and saw three of the creatures feasting on a body nearby.

Without hesitation, Emilia picked up a backpack and drew an axe from the side, using it to attack the creatures, who seemed bloated after eating and shying from the sunlight.

She killed them and dragged their corpses to the hole, tossing them down.

Emilia saw what was left of Hans below and said a quick prayer for his soul.

Then she did a quick search and found what she was looking for: the explosives they'd brought with them in order to blast through solid rock if need be.

She'd watched the team in preparations in the beginning explain how to properly use it, and she decided the only way to end this was to collapse the tunnel and hopefully kill all of the monsters.

Emilia put all of the explosives around the void and wired it all up. She thought she heard the creatures coming up the ropes and she cut them loose, tossing them down.

A creature popped its head up and Emilia slammed it with the flat side of the axe, knocking it back down.

Now she worked quickly, and had it all wired up.

I did this. I shall have to pay for all of these deaths, Emilia thought.

She'd been trying to ignore all of the bodies of her team all around her.

Emilia detonated the charges and ran as the ground began to collapse all around her.

She staggered for a few feet as the dirt and rocks shifted and she closed her eyes as she began to stumble and fall.

CHAPTER FORTY-SEVEN

Dieter needed to apologize, really apologize, to Greta before they were both killed. He knew it was going to be the end very soon, too.

The creatures were pacing with them, like they were playing with their food.

Dieter knew from what he'd already seen the two of them were going to be nothing more than food.

"I want to reiterate how sorry I am," Dieter said to Greta.

"What? Are you really going to do this now? We need to escape."

Dieter stopped and shook his head. "We're not getting out of this. Look."

Up ahead there were dozens of the creatures, waiting for the pair.

Greta stopped and gripped Dieter's arm. "Then, for what it's worth, I accept your apology. You were a jerk and you ruined my career… except you didn't, because I could have raised my chin and moved forward. Instead, I used the negative to destroy my career, I blamed you for every shortcoming, every misstep I did myself."

"I was so stupid. I was jealous of you and I was in love with you, truth be told," Dieter said and smiled faintly. "I thought, maybe someday…"

Greta shook her head. "Maybe if you hadn't done it we could've been true friends, like what you have with Emilia."

Dieter groaned. "What do you think will happen to Emilia? Hopefully she doesn't come down here."

"Hopefully no one ever comes down here, because treasure train or no treasure train, this is a giant graveyard filled with ghouls," Greta said.

Dieter saw the ghouls were getting closer, inch by inch, all around them. Even from the ceiling now, too. Waiting to get into position to pounce, perhaps.

"What do you think they really are? How long have they been down here? What do they survive on? So many questions that we'll never get the answer to," Greta said.

"Maybe we'll get the answers when we meet our Maker." Dieter didn't know if he believed in a higher power or if Greta did, but he supposed now was a good time to start believing and hope his soul would be saved.

"I won't be able to fight them off for long," Greta said.

"You and me both." Dieter wrapped his arms around Greta and pulled her in close. He was glad she didn't resist. "So… friends only, then? I always thought we had a spark between us."

"You were sadly mistaken," Greta said with a laugh. "In another parallel universe, you and I would be the best of friends. Working on papers and projects together."

Dieter chuckled. "Yeah, I guess you're right. I hope there is another universe where Emilia gets her wish and finds the treasure without complications and is able to re-distribute the wealth back to the rightful families. She becomes a national hero and her name is mentioned for years and years to come."

Greta put her head on Dieter's chest. "Yes, I want to live in that universe."

Dieter felt the first claw rip across the back of his calf and felt Greta shudder against him as she was attacked.

They cried out once or twice each before they were ripped apart, still holding onto one another.

CHAPTER FORTY-EIGHT

The creature was thrown to the ground when everything exploded around him.

When it finally came to, part of the mountain was gone.

The others were all dead, parts of their bodies scattered across the ground as far as it could smell.

The intruders had done this. Entered their world, their safe place, where they had lived and thrived for so long.

A large void replaced where their home had been.

What now? Time to find a new place to live. Time to see if there were more of its kind under the mountain in other spots.

Time to eat and survive.

The one who had done this, had destroyed their home, was still alive. Still breathing but only barely.

It wanted to slice the neck open and drink the blood. Feast on the flesh.

But there were noises in the distance getting louder.

More of these monsters were coming to finish it off, unless it was able to escape.

It rushed away, up what was left of the mountain, hoping to escape another attack.

CHAPTER FORTY-NINE

Emilia was lying in the hospital bed in pain. Her legs had been broken, her right arm useless. Ribs had been crushed and she had internal bleeding.

Several operations over the past week had stabilized her, and she was awake and aware.

Aware everyone else on the expedition was dead.

Dieter and Greta. Roger. Hans. All of them.

The police had taken her statement about what had happened but they seemed skeptical, until a few moments ago.

Photos of the creatures had been shown to her by a spokesperson.

"This will hit the news by the morning, and it will be quite the shock," Emilia was told.

Emilia knew the train had also been found, along with more bodies. All of the people working with her were dead. The explosives had not only collapsed the void below her feet, but it had sent ripples up and down the mountain and collapsed other spots where her teams were working.

Everyone is dead because of me, Emilia thought.

She never told the authorities about Hans Koch and why he was really there, omitting his part in all of this except for his sacrifice so she could go free. What would it matter at this point? The treasure had been found, mostly intact, and the Polish authorities were going to make sure it got to the right people. The families and museums it had been stolen from.

Emilia felt like there was some good that had come out of all of this. Her mission had been successful in that fact, at least.

"Are any of the monsters still alive?" Emilia asked a few days later, once she was well enough to sit up in bed.

"No. They're all dead. Every last one."

Emilia hoped that was true, and also wondered if there were other colonies of them underground. She'd inadvertently discovered a new species, and she was told several of them had been collected for further study.

"There are many news agencies from around the world that want to speak with you."

Emilia shook her head. She wasn't ready to talk about this, might never be ready.

She felt sad more than anything.

Emilia felt truly alone.

As long as they are all gone, I can eventually rest easy, she thought.

Until then, she steered clear of the news on the television and began to heal, physically if not mentally.

Her friends and colleagues were all dead.

The End

www.ingramcontent.com/pod-product-compliance
Lightning Source LLC
Chambersburg PA
CBHW061243170626
46809CB00007B/2808
9781923165687